AN ALIEN LORE

CALLA ZAE

PROSE & CONCEPTS

AN ALIEN LORE

SOLDIERS OF SAEDO 5

USA TODAY BESTSELLING AUTHOR

CALLA ZAE

COPYRIGHT

An Alien Lore

Copyright © 2021 by Calla Zae

Cover Art Copyright: Calla Zae

Space Map Art Copyright: Calla Zae

Prose & Concepts LLC

210 Park Avenue, Suite #280

Worcester, MA 01609

www.proseandconcepts.com

Library of Congress Cataloging-in-Publication Data

Library of Congress Control Number: 2021943999

First edition Ebook ISBN: 978-1-952820-18-2

First edition Paperback ISBN: 978-1-952820-19-9

Audiobook ISBN: 978-1-952820-20-5

ALARUS GALAXY MAP

PLANET CELERON

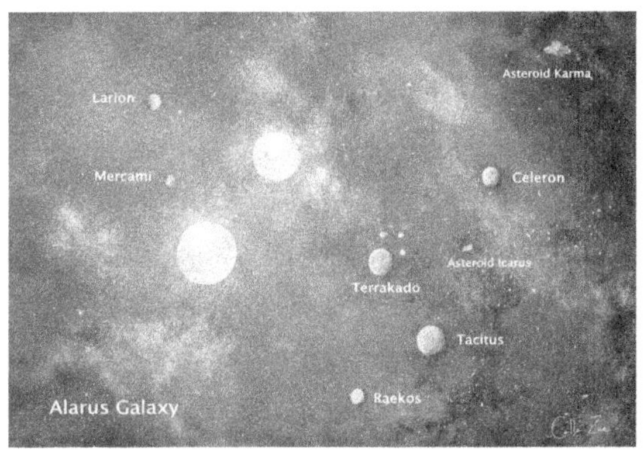

For those who wish upon a star.

.

.

.

"To love someone is to identify with them."
—*Aristotle*

ONE

R‍ITA PLACED an order for two more Book Arrangers for the Village Library. These BAs were robotic bookcases that could transform into ladders or stepping stools, making it easier for her and her coworkers to retrieve, transport, and organize books.

As she checked that task off her to-do list, she strode by the Archives Room. The dullness in the room caught her eye.

"Where's the glow from the Sacred Tablet?" Rita muttered to herself as she scanned her face on the screen before entering.

She gasped when she glanced at the empty, wooden shelf that normally housed the Sacred Tablet of Saedo. A rectangular shape of dust outlined where the tablet had been sitting. Energy pulsed from the emptiness, but there was no glow, not even a hint of it. About eight inches wide and ten inches long, the glassy tablet was made from the Saedonite stone, a rare brown crystal that radiated a bright glow to the entire room.

Where did it go? Nerves churned in her stomach. Though the slate was blank to the eye, she was told it held sacred stories that revealed themselves only when the tablet decided it was time to the right person. Rita had stared at it a few times, but nothing was disclosed to her.

With urgency, she walked around the Archives Room, checking on other sacred books and artifacts; nothing else was missing. The Sacred Tablet was the most precious item in the room. Questions bombarded her. Did someone steal it? When? How and who?

Rita rushed out to the front desk and found Valda, her long-legged coworker with wiry orange hair. "We have a problem."

"What do you mean?" Valda put down an old book. It had pages made from refined dirt and wood that were processed by the powerful energies of the two suns on planet Celeron.

"The Sacred Tablet is missing. I noticed it when I walked by. Did you move it?"

"No, I know better than to move stuff in that room. The tablet belongs on that shelf, where it's been forever." Valda pulled up a virtual screen from the desk. "Let me look through the recordings. The camera must have caught something."

Rita thought back and remembered her sister, Vanessa, had stopped by a few days ago with her lover, Arkon, to retrieve copies of some Saedo texts. Those originals were still in the Archives Room. Did Vanessa and Arkon accidentally take it? They wouldn't do that. They knew better.

But she messaged Vanessa to double check anyway.

Hey, did you take the Sacred Tablet home by accident? It's not in the Archives Room.

A quick reply splashed on Rita's screen. *No. We have plenty to read from the copies you gave us. Something wrong?*

Fear bubbled in Rita's gut. She didn't want to alarm her sister, who had gone through enough already. Vanessa and Arkon recently fought off a bunch of nasty worm-like creatures, called squirmurs, that attacked the province during the alien storm.

Nothing to worry about. We're reorganizing the library. Maybe it was moved somewhere. Chat later. Gotta go.

Vanessa had a sixth sense about things and the longer Rita chatted with her, the more she'd pick up that something was off. Vanessa had a new restaurant to focus on right now.

"The only visitors were Vanessa and Arkon. Everything looks normal." Valda fast-forwarded the recording. "Right here, we can see the tablet on the shelf. What's the airy thing that's floating around? It's making the images blurry, dulling the room. No one came in or out of that room. This *is* strange."

An uncomfortable feeling settled in Rita. "I know the Sacred Tablet is important to Saedo, but I've never seen what's on it. Have you?"

Valda shook her head, anxiety furrowed between her orange eyebrows. "No. Not many have seen the texts. I think Grandma Ova has, but I'm not sure about anyone else. The tablet contains sacred data to Saedo. It was discovered a long time ago after an earthquake shifted the land. A farmer discovered it in the soil because of its glow."

"We have to notify the authorities." Though Rita didn't know what was on the tablet, she considered its importance like the Constitution of the United States. "I'll alert Chief Mozar's office. Can you inform Kairon for me? Just brief her and let her know we have everything under control. I don't want to ruin her vacation with worry. There's nothing she can do about it."

"Sure." Valda glanced at her smart pendant, dangling from her necklace. "I've got an appointment in thirty minutes. I'll inform her on my way out." She grabbed her sparkling purse. "Will you be okay here? Lerma and I will be in tomorrow morning. You should close up soon too."

"I will. See you tomorrow."

Kairon was the main librarian who had hired Rita, giving her a job to start a new life in Saedo. Even though the disappearance of the tablet wasn't her fault, she had a responsibility to find it. She worked at the Village Library and was responsible for anything that happened in it.

She loved stories, which was why she enjoyed working at the library. Her previous job on Earth was working at a bookstore in an art museum. So she was grateful for this job. It was quiet, allowing her time to heal herself while she delved into stories. The Sacred Tablet held something that drew Rita to it, but she hadn't had time to look at it as much as she'd like to.

Rita had been busy with the reorganization of the new addition, and she was sketching again. She'd abandoned that art for too long, and it was time to remember how it made her happy. But right now, she had to focus on finding the tablet.

What if the missing tablet foreshadowed another threat to Saedo?

Rita contacted Chief Mozar's office, and the representative said she'd relay the message and would send someone to the library soon.

The province was still in the rebuilding mode after the alien storm, so if someone didn't come right away, she'd understand why. There were too many structural damages that needed fixing.

Rita had her own repairs to do and headed to the broken window in her office to start the repair.

TWO

RITA WIPED the sweat trickling down her face as she used the handheld glass-fuser and sealed the cracked glass on the window of her office. She'd finished the two front lobby windows already, so she'd gotten the hang of it. It had been a week since the massive alien storm hit Saedo and damaged properties. Fortunately, the library had received only a few broken windows from flying debris.

It hadn't been a normal storm. It was engineered by the Ulkrins, a star race from the Province of Agarrek. These were also the aliens who abducted Rita and her sisters from Earth on New Year's Eve. If it weren't for the soldiers of Saedo who had rescued her and her sisters, Rita couldn't imagine what would've happened to them. The Ulkrins were known to abduct females to reproduce their young.

Would Rita and her sisters be birthing evil aliens right now if they hadn't been saved? Her body shivered from the thought. She almost dropped the glass-fuser. Why did they need to abduct females? Didn't they have female Ulkrins to mate with? She remembered their grotesque faces and understood why females would stay away.

Did the missing Sacred Tablet have anything to do with the Ulkrins? Did they send a squirmur into the Archives Room? Squirmurs were large worms sent by the Ulkrins that infected the soil in Saedo. The recording didn't show any worms breaking through the floor or walls. Besides, the room was protected by two layers of energy fields that would alarm the security system—which was monitored by the government—if someone had entered without permission or taken something out of the room.

As she worked, her mind wandered to the stunning star-being she'd been secretly sketching for the past five months. It had been a long time since she had been inspired to create art. Jarzell became her excuse to draw again.

She recalled when she first met him. It had been chaotic that day when Jarzell and his brothers brought Rita and her sisters to the rescue center to be examined by the doctors. Despite the fear and uncertainty surrounding her at that time, his powerful presence calmed her. The self-assured way he moved and delegated tasks had held her gaze. His handsome green face, the spiky brown hair, and those deep-set gray eyes found a place inside her. It was only a snapshot of him, but that was all she needed to begin sketching again. They never saw each other after that day.

She missed a few dinner invitations to Emma and Raeko's house, where a lot of soldiers gathered to eat and hang out. Her oldest sister fell for Raeko during the rescue. Their instant love proved that fate worked in wonders.

Rita's body shivered from imagining Jarzell's face. No one knew about her secret crush, not even her sisters. It wasn't really a crush; he was an art project that intrigued her. Every artist needed a source of inspiration.

Jarzell was her muse; an attractive green star-being that motivated her in private, and that was how he would remain forever. He probably didn't even know she existed. Why would someone like him be interested in someone like her? Her ex-boyfriend, Philip, had loved to remind her of her flaws. The flaws were etched in her mind the same way they were etched on her back.

Years ago, she had thought Philip was the love of her life. But she'd gotten a reality check when she discovered him in bed with one of her friends. Her friendship ended that day, along with her relationship.

That betrayal knifed deep, the blade cutting into her heart and through her back, ripping open her scars. Once again, she was reminded she wasn't worthy of love.

Despite that, Rita believed there was more for her. She still clung to that belief now. She was raised better than that; she was raised to never give up. On this new planet that had shown her unimaginable things, she'd begun to believe anything was possible. That even someone as flawed as her could find peace and happiness.

You sound pathetic, Rita. Enough.

Rita scolded herself for giving Philip even an ounce of her time. She shifted her thoughts to finding the missing tablet. Where could it be?

Rita had no doubt the Ulkrins were planning another attack. Vanessa, who had a sixth sense, also felt something approaching, which was why she had retrieved some history books for research.

The Sacred Tablet was a blank slate to everyone, and there was no replica of it. What was on it? And why was it missing now? Valda mentioned that Grandma Ova had seen the words on the tablet. Rita made a mental note to ask her. She'd never met this wise old star-being, but heard so much from her sisters, who had met her.

Rita sealed up the last crack and climbed down the ladder.

This temporary patch would keep the windowpanes intact until a professional could repair the windows. Cracked windows weren't a priority compared to the other damages in Saedo. Something had kept Saedo's citizens safe during that dangerous storm. Rita had a feeling that the missing tablet had something to do with it.

Rita didn't have the sixth sense like Vanessa, but she had an intuition. She was an artist, and she was good at tuning into her feelings. She had been good at it before Philip marred her confidence. A cracked heart couldn't function and, therefore, lost its ability to tune in to anything. But living here in Saedo, Rita was connecting to herself again; slowly, but surely. She was regaining her "reception" to the Universe. The satellite within herself expanded its frequency, if that made any sense.

When Rita got off the robotic ladder, it transformed back into a compact bookcase and stood beside her with locked wheels. The small Book Arranger that she called Little BA-11, along with other BAs, helped run the library smoothly.

A trickle of sweat streamed down her back. She took off her lightweight cardigan, made from the light-trek fabric that adjusted to body temperature. It wasn't cooling her right now. Why was that? It had always worked before. She gulped down a bottle of blue water, and it cooled her a little.

Why was she so fricking hot? The tank top she wore didn't help much.

She strode to an undamaged small window and opened it. A gust of cool air entered, cooling her. She glanced at her smart bracelet. It was already four in the afternoon, and she still had a lot of work on her to-do list. Everyone had gone home because the Village Library had adopted new operational hours until the windows were fixed.

She should probably head out soon. She'd been working non-stop this week, which was probably why her body heated up. Despite that, she could use the quiet space to add details to her sketch of him. Sketching relaxed her. She'd been having trouble with his eyes. She couldn't seem to get them right. They lacked life, but that was because she needed another look at him. When she could perfect the eyes in her drawing, she'd be comfortable moving on to a painting of him.

More sweat trickled down her forehead. Maybe she shouldn't have patched up the cracked windowpanes, but she didn't want a glass panel to fall on her or her coworkers unexpectedly. She'd soldered jewelry pieces when she was in college studying art, so using a glass-glue gun wasn't that difficult.

A jolt of heat sizzled down her spine, and a flash of fire popped into her vision. She closed her eyes and dimmed the flame. It disappeared from her mind without making her panic. This technique had helped her cope with the trauma of the car accident that had burned part of her back, scarring her and changing her forever. Living here made it easier to deal with that memory.

Heat and fire had never bothered her until that fateful accident. It was true what they said about trauma affecting your entire body. Hers remembered the fear, the smell of burned leather, and the snapping sound of the angry fire. The pain that scorched her skin, and the fact that death was just a breath away, all seeped into her psyche, making her shudder. But living in Saedo had allowed her to release that trauma at her own pace.

She'd read in healing books that fear rose to the surface before it could be discharged. Could the strange heat in her body be a sign of release? Or was it impending illness?

Please don't get sick, she muttered to herself. She had too much to do and couldn't afford the time off. She had a missing tablet to search for on top of everything else. The new addition to the library had to be furnished and organized before the grand opening. She retrieved the care kit from the storage room, and pulled out the handheld body-reader, which was a six-inch crystal wand that read body temperature like a thermometer from Earth.

At the touch of the clear quartz, a field of energy embraced her in an enormous bubble. A virtual screen popped up with a scan of her body's temperature.

"What?" Rita looked at the crystal wand body-reader. "This is weird." Had it malfunctioned? She tested it three times. Each time the screen showed the normal human body temperature range between 97 to 99 degrees Fahrenheit.

What the hell is going on?

Rita placed the body-reader wand back into the care kit and returned to her office. If she wasn't hot, why would she sweat? She'd have to try it again when she got home.

Living in Saedo heightened her sensitivity. Even her sisters could feel energy more now than when they were on Earth. Being in an eighth-dimensional matrix of Saedo lifted them from the density of Earth. That was what she'd learned from reading the books about various planets and energy fields.

A chime from the front door startled her. *Shit.* She'd forgotten to close and lock up after Valda left.

Rita strode out to the front desk, and her heart galloped. Her muse stood in the middle of the main room, wandering around and looking at the disarray of books on tables, bookcases, and stacked chairs.

Like a fool, she froze, staring at Jarzell from behind the desk. He was even more attractive than she remembered. He wore a short-sleeve black knit top that hugged his body and showed off every taut muscle. How could a body have that much bulk on it? A pair of light-washed high-tech denim elongated his athletic physique. He surveyed the ceiling and strode over to the window she had patched. His hand ran over the cracked section she'd sealed.

He probably wondered who had done such a sloppy job. Insecurity rose up inside her. She thought being on a new planet would eradicate that feeling once and for all. But that thorn of self-doubt was rooted deep inside her; it pricked her unexpectedly. When would she be able to yank it out?

She glanced at her bare arms and scolded herself. She shouldn't have taken her cardigan off and left it in her office. What if he saw the scars on her back? The tank top she wore wasn't revealing or anything, but she felt exposed.

She shouldn't care what he thought of her. He didn't know her, and she didn't know him. She only knew him from an image in her mind. And like anything in the mind, it grew into its own thing.

After that car accident, she became a woman who wrapped herself in uncertainty and depression. It took her a long time to realize she wasn't blemished. But acknowledging that and *believing* it were two different things. That ghost of insecurity frightened her when she least expected it, especially when standing next to a perfect man.

Why don't you wear something to cover your scars? People are going to stare, and that's going to embarrass me.

Philip's words bounced in her head. She hated the fact that she couldn't erase his words from her mind. Damn him.

Who's going to buy this rubbish? Her chest ached at the memory of his criticism of her work. She shrank a little.

Splatters of paint won't feed you. Stop painting. Get a real job. You have bills to pay, and I won't support your foolish dream.

Rita's hand went to her chest as she attempted to calm the internal storm whirling inside. Philip hadn't always been supportive of her artistic endeavors, but he only became brutally blunt after... after she'd obtained the scars. The pain caused by a man who once said he loved her was too much at this moment.

She stared at Jarzell, who stood with his back to her. Any imagination of him took a step back from the pain and pity. The vow she'd made to herself that no man would hurt her again surfaced like a tidal wave that overwhelmed all other emotion. She closed her eyes, taking a deep breath.

When she opened her eyes, she straightened her shoulders, clearing her throat. "The library is closed now."

Jarzell whirled around. He surveyed her for a while, or was that just her confused mind seeing things that weren't true? She couldn't trust herself right now. She should've stopped Philip's intrusion when she first sensed it. Now he had ruined her day. *Bastard.*

Jarzell strode up to the front desk. Was that a spark in his gray eyes? For a moment, she forgot her irritation.

"Then why is the door unlocked?" He jerked his chin toward the door.

Where had her mind gone today? Rita pressed a button on the desk, which locked the door. "Pardon me, I forgot to lock it."

The irritated feeling returned and clawed down her skin. But she couldn't stop studying the details of his face. Those powerful gray eyes had a rim of aqua around the irises. A slight angle that could be seen from up close made him look like a tiger. This man with the dark green skin had an angular face where shadows and light played beautifully. He captivated her like a Monet painting. She stared into his eyes, trying to capture their essence so she could sketch them.

Feeling awkward, Rita forced herself to look away and pretended to organize the books on her desk. "How can I help you?"

Jarzell eyed her, and a ripple of energy brushed against her skin.

"I remember you," he said in a deep and hypnotic voice.

"You're Rita, one of the Nelson sisters. We rescued you from the Ulkrins."

He remembers my name.

Joy burst in the pit of her stomach. His face graced several pages of her sketchbook. When she first drew him, it was just instinct. She had never met a star-being before, and suddenly being on a new planet with aliens and other creatures baffled and excited her. That excitement sparked her creativity. Jarzell possessed an unforgettable face that had evolved into something more. She was still trying to figure out what that "more" was.

If he ever saw her sketchbook, would he find it creepy she had so many drawings of his face? She'd be too embarrassed to show him or anyone else. How would she explain herself? She'd make sure he'd never see it.

"Yes, I'm Rita. Thank you for saving us that day."

The soldiers of Saedo were the elite police force for the province. They were multi-talented and possessed various skills that supported all the citizens. While they worked with Chief Mozar on government business, they built homes and worked in cybersecurity on the Galacto Net—which was like a massive internet for the galaxy. They were also involved with city planning, trade negotiations, and so much more.

The Saedo citizens had welcomed Rita and her sisters into their province, and gave them jobs that enabled the siblings to live as permanent residents. She owed them so much gratitude for the new beginning she desperately wanted.

Everyone needed a second chance. At the end of the day, what mattered was her family and her heart. Her only family was her sisters, and they wanted to start fresh as well.

Saedo became the breath of fresh air to start her healing journey. The scars on her back tightened from her memories, and she shifted her feet, not wanting him to see her discomfort.

Why was he still looking at her?

"You're welcome. I'm Jarzell. Chief Mozar mentioned the Sacred Tablet is missing. I've been assigned to this investigation. I would've come sooner, but I was helping Maeson repair the buildings down at the Village Center. I saw your sister, Sasha, dropping off some food for him."

Sasha had a crush on Maeson and tracked him down to let him know her feelings a few months ago. Now, they lived happily together in the home he built for them.

"That's fantastic news. I was wondering when someone would stop by. Come with me." Rita led him to the Archive Room.

Jarzell fell into step with her, and her body's temperature increased. She prayed she wouldn't sweat. It was a different kind of heat, not the odd one that made her sweat earlier. This heat bloomed from her stomach, stirring up all kinds of feelings she hadn't dared look at after her relationship ended with Philip.

Was this sudden emergence of heat a product of her imagination? Her imagination was a world of its own. She reveled in it, but she also feared it because it could produce illusions that weren't safe to believe.

With Jarzell's presence so close, she got a whiff of a pleasant and musky scent from him, and her body wanted to move closer. She remained a professional and ignored it.

Rita concentrated on the task at hand, scanned her face on the screen outside of the Archives Room, and gestured for him to do the same. "The security alarm records who enters the room."

They stepped on a wooden floor and entered the space filled with ancient books and slabs of stones with etchings on them. Light green walls wrapped around the room. The atmosphere made her feel like she had stepped into a quiet forest or something. Energy hummed around her as it flowed from one bookcase to the next. The scent of old books snuck up her nose, making her think she was inhaling ancient wisdom.

She pointed to the empty shelf. "The tablet is missing from here."

His forehead wrinkled. "Maybe the Saedo lore is true…"

"What do you mean?"

"Some say the Sacred Tablet has its own consciousness. When it goes missing, it's a sign that something…"

She'd read up on several Saedo lore, and they intrigued her. But she hadn't encountered anything about the Sacred Tablet. She'd been into mystical and weird things since she was a child. It was part of the reason why she studied the arts. She saw things differently, and art was the only way she could truly express herself.

His eyes flared with a new intensity that tugged at some invisible thread in her stomach. The gray took on a new shade, making him appear dangerous and mysterious at the same time. The rims of aqua had disappeared.

"Something what?" Rita asked.

"Something perilous is brewing in Saedo." He paused for a moment. "Someone took the tablet to harm Saedo. We must find it."

THREE

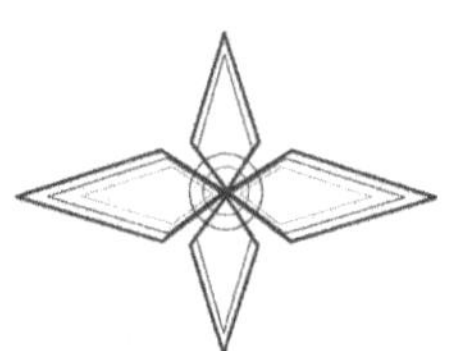

"But I checked all the cameras," Rita said. "No one has entered the Archive Room for months."

"There are other means of getting to things without being seen."

Could someone have infiltrated the government's security system? Or did he mean something else? She was on planet Celeron, where technology was more advanced than that on Earth and magical things occurred every day.

"Do you mean someone manipulated the security system, entered the room, and took the tablet without being caught? But what about the energetic protective fields? Shouldn't those have alerted your office or something?"

"Your mind works fast. It's efficient. I like it."

His voice was edged with something that excited her. The excitement perplexed her. When was the last time she reacted this way with a man?

"Yes, and no. I mean, if an enemy wanted to steal a tablet, he or she with the right powers could infiltrate anything. But there could be another energy at play here. Let's have a look around the room."

Jarzell pressed something on his black wristband, and light fanned out, scanning for energy. Rita rounded the corner to the old books section where the pages of pressed dirt and wood created a lovely earthly scent. She stepped forward and a panel of glass from a nearby window shattered on the floor.

"Flekken! Are you okay?" Jarzell nudged her behind him without hesitation. The simple movement did something to her. When was the last time a man automatically protected her like that? Even during her good days with Philip, he'd never showed this kind of protection for her.

What had she been missing?

"I'm fine." Her fear that the panels would shatter had come true. "I guess I missed these two windows on my to-do list." She didn't know why she forgot to check the Archives Room for any damages.

Jarzell glanced up at the windows that needed replacing. "Why aren't the windows fixed? How many broken windows are in the library?" His tone carried an edge of disbelief.

"Because everyone is busy rebuilding and working on stuff that has greater priority than window replacements. We submitted the repairs to whoever is available. There are twelve windows if you count the two in this room."

Jarzell cursed and checked his smart wristband. A virtual screen popped up in the air with a list of pending repairs. He moved the items on the list around. "I'll take that task." He tapped more buttons and looked at her. "I just placed an order for new glass panels. They should arrive tomorrow."

Rita admired his efficiency. "You can just move things around like that? Don't you need to let anyone know?"

"Besides being a soldier for Saedo, I'm also the Delegator in times of need. I oversee the overall urgency of the province and delegate tasks to help organize and expedite the process. Right now, I deem these cracked windowpanes hazardous. They're not small, and they're situated in all the main hallways, reading rooms, and offices placing everyone in danger. That elevates everything." With his dark boots, he maneuvered the shards together for easy cleanup. "You could've been hurt."

That was the soldier in him speaking, the man who had a capacity to care for others besides himself. She hadn't met that many men in her life, and the considerate ones she had met were all taken. If Jarzell showed this kind of concern for someone he hardly knew, that meant he had a good conscience, right?

What would he do for someone who captured his heart?

Wait a minute, why is she thinking about him like that?

This had been an odd day, indeed. From the sudden disappearance of the Sacred Tablet to the strange heat in her body, and now to her inexplicable reaction and thoughts about Jarzell. Her mind struggled for logic, for anything that would make sense.

When she had a quiet moment, she'd sit down and think about everything. Rita activated the robotic cleaner that rolled over and swept the shards of glass from the floor, dumping them into its wide mouth.

Ever since she had started sketching again, she tapped into that part of herself that was all heart and soul. She supposed she needed to connect to herself better so she could remember how to differentiate what was real and what wasn't.

Rita shook her head at how she'd let one man crumple her. Like a crumpled piece of paper, she was ironing herself out.

Jarzell moved around the room, taking notes on the virtual screen as he went along. He moved with swiftness and efficiency. When he reached for a book on the top shelf, his muscles flexed, and her stomach flipped. His whole body was all muscle and man, and she found herself imagining other parts of him.

Shit, shit, shit!

Rita scolded herself for the brief entertainment, but stopped. This was *her life*, her mind. She could live however she wanted; imagine whatever she liked. No one had control of what lurked in her brain. So she continued her private illustration of him while he moved around the room. She rendered him with broad strokes, taking in the clean lines of his long body. The other details could be sprinkled in later. In an attempt to look occupied instead of ogling at him, she ran a hand over the empty shelf where the tablet had been. Energy zapped her fingers, and she retracted her hand.

Too occupied with whatever he was doing, he didn't notice the strange energy zap she just experienced. He stalked from one section of the room to another, collecting data.

"I did a quick scan of the room, and didn't pick up any new power source," he said, tapping at the screen that splashed a set of codes she didn't understand. His concentration was focused on his task, unwavering from all distractions. He appeared like someone who gave his all and probably expected the same in return.

For someone who delegated urgent matters, he no doubt favored impatience over patience, preferring urgency over slowness.

Jarzell's wristband buzzed and Arkon's face appeared on the screen. Vanessa and Arkon had fallen in love during the alien storm when they were attacked by the squirmurs.

"We got some data from the squirmur's device. You need to see what we discovered. You available now? I'm at the research center. If you want to wait until—"

"I'll be there in a few minutes." Jarzell pulled up another screen, showing a calendar filled with information.

"That's what I thought. Promptness is your forte."

"There's nothing wrong with that. I know when something's

urgent. Impatience is an excellent weapon if you know how to use it. See you soon." Jarzell swiped to another screen, typed something, and clicked it off.

The busy energy that emanated from Jarzell twisted her stomach uncomfortably. For a moment, that overloaded energy reminded her of Philip when he had been too occupied with work.

Was she walking down a familiar path and didn't know it? Besides the handsome face and the way his presence pulled at her, why was she attracted to Jarzell? Could it be that her subconscious recognized a familiar trait? Was Jarzell a test to her healing?

Was he a copy of Philip that hadn't fully revealed itself?

The thought made her ill. Rita wasn't the same person who had flinched from Philip's criticism. She was now a stronger woman, who had developed a powerful armor to protect herself.

Jarzell fascinated her on another level, one she didn't fully understand yet. Regardless, she had to be extra careful now that she'd seen a familiar trait that brought on bitter memories.

She vowed never to repeat that mistake again. One mistake had taken her a long time to heal. She didn't want to go backward. Rita Nelson only faced forward now.

"I've got to take care of an urgent matter." Jarzell walked up to her and opened his mouth to say something else, but closed it.

Something flickered in his eyes. She desperately wanted to know what he was thinking. For some damn reason, this man ignited a desire in her that had been dormant for a long time. She hadn't been with a man since Philip. No one had interested her. No one until Jarzell. There was nothing wrong with attraction. She understood the arts and appreciated beauty. But she had to take cautious steps now.

Jarzell was a gorgeous star-being, and she was certain the females in Saedo agreed. Was he with someone? Geez, she hadn't considered that. He *had* to be with someone. He was too perfect not to be.

Still, that didn't stop her sexy imagination. Though she knew it wasn't good for the long haul, it was fine for temporary satisfaction. She could enjoy pretending her muse wanted to be with her, scars and all. Residing in her mind was her forte.

"What's that peeking out?" Jarzell veered toward her back.

The unexpected comment shut Rita down, including the wild imagination that had given her joy a moment ago. He saw her scars, or part of them. She didn't want him to see her like that. She wasn't ready for anyone to see her in that way.

Why did she take off her cardigan?

How should she reply? She didn't want him inquiring because she didn't want to talk about her past.

But as she stood inches from Jarzell, her skin tingled. "Just an old scar." She wrapped her arms around herself in a protective gesture and changed the subject. "What do you think your brothers have discovered from the squirmur?"

His eyebrows quirked at her segue, but he didn't press on. "Whatever it is, I hope it'll help us eradicate those damn Ulkrins."

She didn't know which was more important, the newly discovered data from the squirmurs or the missing Sacred Tablet. "Do you have everything you need from the Archives Room?"

Jarzell checked his wristband. "I'm all set. Don't worry, the Sacred Tablet is my priority right now." He headed to the door and stopped. "I'll be back tomorrow to install your new windows. After that, I'll start my search." He smiled, and warmth swelled in her chest. "I'm glad I finally got to meet you."

What did that mean? Was she reading too much into a simple sentence? Maybe he just meant that he was glad to meet her, just like how she was glad to have finally seen her muse in person again. But a quiet part of her yearned for his statement to mean something more.

She hadn't felt this kind of longing in a long time. Was that why her body was reacting in strange ways? It didn't know what to do either.

Ugh. Stop analyzing, Rita. Go home, take a bath, and go to bed.

She huffed a breath at her practical self and agreed. Given the bizarre day, she was probably doing too much of everything from feeling too much to thinking too much.

She had to clear her mind so she could recover the missing tablet.

FOUR

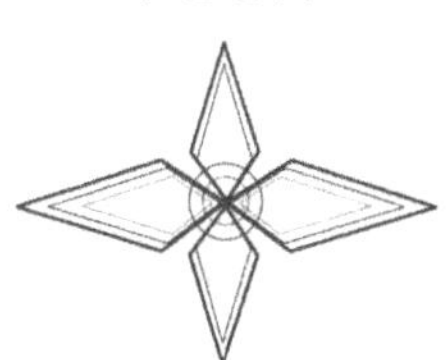

RITA SUBMERGED her body in the warm water inside an amethyst crystal bathtub with lilac salt. Long strands of her purple hair flowed like delicate water serpents. Colorful gallica rose petals tipped with glittering edges floated around the tub, and a sweet aroma filled the room, relaxing her. The petals moved, creating a slight current that massaged her muscles from underneath the water.

Though the water soothed her, she couldn't shake the unsettled feeling of the day. The strange heat that couldn't be detected by the body-reader lingered in her. It sat at the bottom of her tummy, simmering. How did she know that? She had no idea. It was like an invisible voice snuck a clue into her ear.

The heat baffled and scared her. Who wouldn't be terrified? Heat reminded her of fire, and fire gave her the scars. Some people said that she was lucky to escape the car fire with just wounds on her back. The drunk driver who had slammed into her wasn't so lucky. If it hadn't been for the large cedar tree that stopped her car, she would've rolled down some embankment, and who knew what would've happened.

A shudder rippled through her at the memory, and she

inhaled deep breaths, reminding herself that she was safe. She recalled how the fire seeped into her skin. How the pain had reverberated through her entire body, and how she had thought she was going to die. She'd never forget that feeling. An off-duty firefighter pulled her out with the help of a Good Samaritan.

Though she was grateful to have survived, the pain and depression that followed were worse. She felt ugly, useless, damaged, and unworthy. At least, that was what her mind and her ex-boyfriend had made her believe. Her siblings tried to help her, but she believed Philip. Love made people blind and irrational. She had wasted so much time and energy on a man who had never loved her at all.

Being in Saedo allowed her to accept everything as it was, even the heat. But this was a different kind of heat. There was something else attached to it. She couldn't explain it.

It was as though this unfamiliar heat was "befriending" her. Strange as that may have sounded, that was what she felt. She didn't fear it. It didn't harm her, and she didn't feel pain from the heat, just a minor discomfort. But even the discomfort had subsided significantly compared to this morning.

This heat wanted her attention. That she knew. When she concentrated on it, the heat lessened. She used her own body-reader when she got home and it had produced the same result: normal body temperature. That confirmed that this warmth in her was something unique.

Jarzell's appearance added to the weird concoction of the day. He was the new paint color that added texture and substance to her quiet and mundane life. She adored her simple lifestyle on planet Celeron in the Alarus galaxy. There was so much to do, see, and learn. More than anything, it created a much-needed distance between her and her past. Everyone needed to heal, and distance and time were the required remedies. Rita was healing in her own way, at her own pace.

But this recent yearning piqued her interest. It had been over a year since her relationship had ended. Did she want to start a relationship now? Was she even ready? She didn't have a straightforward answer to those questions. All she knew was that her heart was whispering something that made her look at Jarzell.

But then again, was she looking at him because he was her artistic muse from the beginning? Or was she attracted to him because of something more? Or was she just a desperate woman who needed companionship because she hadn't been with a man for a while? At the moment, she was acting like a sexually deprived woman.

Oh, God. She kicked at the rose petals playfully, as if she was kicking at her irrationality. Water splashed and the petals continued creating gentle currents in the tub.

Why was she confusing the hell out of herself? This warm bath was supposed to clear her mind, not muddle it.

Rita blew out a breath of frustration, got out of the bathtub, and activated a quick-spray to wash off the salt and clean her hair. The purple dye from her hair would be cleansed in a few days, revealing her naturally brown color. Unlike the hair dyes on Earth, the innovative dyes in Saedo were odorless, non-toxic, and didn't dry out her hair. She loved how they washed off in a couple of weeks for her to try a new color. She'd need to make an appointment with Sasha. Her sister worked at the Color Spectrum salon, and had become one of Saedo's favorite stylists.

Rita looked at herself in the mirror on the shower wall. What color should she choose next to compliment her brown eyes? Jarzell's mesmerizing gray eyes popped into her vision. They held so much life and power. She'd sketch him tonight.

She'd never been more motivated to work on her art than when she landed in the Province of Saedo. If that was any indication that she'd made the right decision to remain on this planet, that was it. Her creativity had taken a backseat after her relationship ended. She had no desire to create or make anything, but being here had made all the difference. No one knew her in Saedo. Being here was like touching a brand-new canvas with no residue of the past. Returning to her creative nature was required for her healing journey.

If she improved her art, maybe she could one day display it at the StoryArt Gallery in the Village Center. Rita had walked by that gallery and admired the paintings and sculptures from artists in Saedo and the nearby provinces. These star-beings were so imaginative; they inspired her to better herself. Another sign that Rita was healing was the courage to even *think* about submitting her work. On Earth, she never thought she was good enough. That self-doubt had prevented her from doing so many things.

Rita shoved all unhappy thoughts away and dressed in her silk nightgown. It was made from purple gallica rose petals and slipped on like butter, giving her skin an orgasm. The sleepwear was from one of Inga's new lingerie collection. Her sister had found her success and happiness in Saedo after meeting her starmate, Osayik. Inga and Osayik had fought off a mother beast of the creatures that attacked them. This mother beast spoke the universal language, which Rita and her sisters understood from the language translator inside their ears. She could also read the universal language after a doctor activated the language codex within her brain from a beam of energy. The doctor told her that human beings possessed a powerful brain that hadn't been fully activated yet.

So far, four of her sisters had found love after living in Saedo for a short amount of time. Rita didn't dare wonder if she would have that kind of luck. Sometimes when you expected too much, it backfired. For now, she would expect nothing, allowing herself to go with the flow. She used this method when she painted, and now, she applied that to every aspect of her life.

She grabbed her notebook, settled into bed, and flipped to a new page. Her smart bracelet buzzed, and Emma's face popped onto the screen.

"Hey you, Vanessa and I are having a bake-off tomorrow night. We're cooking to help feed all the soldiers and helpers who are working overtime to rebuild the villages," her oldest sister said. "Do you want to come over?"

If she wasn't one person short at work and she didn't have furniture and supplies coming in, she wouldn't mind visiting Emma and Vanessa. They were the best chefs and always had delicious foods. "Kairon is on vacation and I have to help Valda and Lerma move books to the new building. We added a children's section. I'm going to have to pass this time."

"Oh, right. I forgot about the recent addition. I can send some food over to you. Raeko told me about a quick delivery service using droids." Emma showed her a picture of a blue cake with peach icing, and Rita's stomach rumbled. "I'm going to make this cake from a recipe my neighbor gave me. But Vanessa is baking something from her own recipe."

Vanessa was an exceptional chef with her own restaurant opening up any day now. Rita couldn't wait to attend the grand opening of Trust Your Gut.

"Sure, I'll take some food."

"I know everyone's anxious in Saedo. The villagers are worried about what the Ulkrins might do next. We're helping the community by feeding them. It's one less thing they have to worry about. I know Raeko and his brothers are working extra hard to find out more about the Ulkrins."

Rita wondered if Jarzell had discovered anything useful from his meeting with Arkon. "Things are still iffy, so try to be careful wherever you go. We have to be cautious."

"Same to you. I'm sending food to Inga, Nina, and Isabella too. They don't want to go out, especially at night."

"It's safer that way."

When Emma clicked off, Rita leaned into her pillow. She knew the threat of the Ulkrins loomed over everyone, but she didn't want to live in fear. Living in fear meant she was giving away her power. She couldn't have that. She had worked too hard to find a stable ground to stand on. Though danger lurked around her, she had to be extra careful as she continued to live her life.

Rita returned her attention to her sketchbook. With a pencil, she began sketching Jarzell's face. He had fine features that captivated her. When she shaded in his eyes, adding a rim around the irises, they appeared to be looking right at her. Her heart thudded, her skin warmed, and her core twitched. Acknowledging the energy in her bedroom, she set the book down and kept her gaze on the illustration. When a hint of teal mist rose up from the image, Rita blinked. It disappeared just as quickly as it had come.

Was it her imagination? How could mist surface from a piece of sketch paper? The paper was made from a combination of recycled tree bark, leaves, and flowers synthesized under the power of the two suns. There was no moisture in the paper for mist to occur. Rita had witnessed magical phenomena in Saedo before, and she had read up on all kinds of inexplicable events. But it was hard to grasp it when she couldn't *see* it.

Rita tried staring at the image again. "Come back. Show me again."

Nothing happened except for the heat coursing through her, flowing like a warm river inside her. It was subtle, yet distinctive enough for her to notice. This wasn't normal. This was... separate from herself. It didn't make any sense at all. How could something inside her be separate?

"What do you want from me?" she asked as if the heat could reply.

It didn't. Somehow, her body had adjusted itself to this new energy. Her body had become a host to a foreign energy. Though she didn't fear it, she wanted to understand it. Why was it happening to her? And why now?

She wasn't going to find any answers tonight. She had a feeling the answers would come to her when it was time, so she concentrated on her art.

After losing herself in several more sketches, Rita curled up on her side, as she considered what kind of art to start next. She dove into her wild thoughts that included a naked Jarzell. She could attempt to sketch his body from pure imagination. Or she could start a painting of him: her very first painting of a star-being.

Excitement thrilled her as she fell into a dream that left her more frustrated than satisfied.

FIVE

The next day, frustration clung to Rita as she tried to organize her tasks in the Village Library. Her moodiness stemmed from an unpleasant dream where she discovered Jarzell with an attractive female star-being. The raw emotion from the past surfaced like a monster, reminding her of Philip's betrayal. Though there was *nothing* between her and Jarzell, the dream still bothered her. It was just a dream, and besides, what right did she have to be jealous?

Her subconscious mind was probably telling her that Jarzell had a mate and for her to back off.

Maybe she should stop sketching him. The more she drew him, the closer she got to him. It was strange how the art communicated with the artist. There was an intimate connection that couldn't be explained. She glanced over at the two landscape paintings hanging on the wall of the front entrance. The artist had used a monochromatic color palette which made the beautiful mountains look like they were jutting out from the paintings.

She'd never dreamed about any other man and woken up

this unsettled. The heat from yesterday remained in her body, like it belonged there. With this cauldron of irritation stirring in her, she dismissed the heat. She didn't have time to contemplate what it wanted from her.

Right now, maybe it wanted to annoy her.

At the front desk, Rita focused on her work and ordered the Book Arranger, the robotic bookcase, to transport the books to the additional space at the back of the library.

"Yes, ma'am." BA-15 rolled away with three shelves of books.

Rita organized and updated her virtual screen. She placed an order for child-safe chairs and tables for the reading room.

"The computers for the kids' room will arrive in a few hours." Valda tied her orange hair into a ponytail and checked a chart from her tablet. Today, she wore a flowing dress that matched her hair. "I'll set those up when they arrive."

"Thanks," Rita said as heat tugged at her and traveled up her arms, spreading across her chest. What the heck was happening? She glanced at her arms and chest, thinking she'd see inflamed skin, but nothing looked abnormal.

"Are you okay today?" Lerma asked. She had four beautiful blue eyes and white hair braided into a knot on the side. She wore a black suit that contrasted her light-green skin. "You seem unlike yourself."

If her coworkers could sense it, that meant she wasn't hiding her emotions well. She worked in an environment where professionalism was required. No one needed to know she was off-kilter. But Valda and Lerma had become quick friends who welcomed Rita when she first started, teaching and training her about the process and procedure of the Village Library.

Rita blew out a breath and ran a hand through her hair. "Sorry, I'm feeling *odd*, if that makes any sense."

Lerma placed a gentle hand on Rita's arm. "We all have those days. Why don't you take a few days off? You've put in a lot of hours lately. Kairon is on vacation, so we can slack off a bit. Also, we've cut back the hours, and the villagers are still reeling from the previous storm. No one's really going out or visiting the library." She gave Rita a one-arm hug. "We haven't had many visitors. I don't mind because we can focus on furnishing the new addition."

Rita nodded, considering the suggestion. "They're probably waiting for the grand opening of the children's room."

"You were supposed to take a vacation last week. But the storm arrived, and you've pushed it back to next month. Take four days off. Valda and I will cover everything." Lerma tapped her temple with a long finger. "I can't believe the Sacred Tablet is missing. When Valda informed me this morning, I went to review the recording myself. How could it disappear like that?"

"My thoughts exactly," Rita said. Maybe she could use a day off, looking for the Sacred Tablet. Something urged her to look for it. She had no idea where the tablet could be, but intuition tugged at her. At that thought, the heat skimmed down the front of her body and she shivered, catching Lerma's attention.

"Yup, you really need a day off before you get sick." Lerma cocked her head. "Take the time off before I alert Kairon and let her know. She'd force you to stay home."

Rita laughed and appreciated Lerma's concern. "Okay, I'll take four days off starting tomorrow. We have someone coming in to replace the windows today."

"We do?"

Rita slapped a hand on her forehead. She'd forgotten to tell her coworkers? Where had her mind been?

"Shit. Sorry, I thought I told you. I meant to send you and Valda a message yesterday to inform you. One windowpane collapsed in the Archives Room. Luckily, it missed me. Anyway, Jarzell is stopping by to replace them."

"Jarzell?" Lerma's eyebrow arched. "He's a hottie known for his work ethics. He gets things done quickly and efficiently. Boom, boom, boom." She leaned in and whispered. "But I'm curious, does he apply that in bed too?"

Rita gasped, and Lerma laughed. "What? I'm just being honest. I've already got a mate at home. But I know some of my friends have crushes on him."

That intrigued her. "Does he have a mate?"

Lerma shrugged. "I haven't seen him with one, but he travels a lot for Chief Mozar. So maybe she lives in another province?"

Rita's chest tightened at that idea. Why should it matter? He didn't show any interest in her. He only said he was glad to meet her, and she had made up her own meaning to it. If he had slews of females after him, why would he want her?

Still, sadness plopped down and claimed a corner of her heart. It was as if her muse was no longer hers.

Stop it, Rita.

The door chimed, signifying a visitor. Ignoring it, Rita focused on her virtual screen, checking to see what she had to finish before she took the four days off. Heat skated down her arm.

Lerma cleared her throat. "Hi, Jarzell. How's it going?"

Rita whipped her gaze to him.

"Going well, thanks." Jarzell offered a nod, looking handsome in his blue top that showed off his muscular arms, and high-tech denim ripped at the knees. "Is Quern treating you well? If not, you let me know, and I'll have a chat with him."

Lerma laughed. "I'll relay that message to him."

His attention swerved to Rita. "I've got the windowpanes on the longship ready to go. I brought two droids to assist me. It should only take a few hours, so please don't be alarmed with the noises."

She understood what Lerma said about her friends' attraction to him. He was a gorgeous star-being that demanded attention. He smiled, and her stomach flipped. Something flickered in his eyes. His expression softened. Or was that her imagination? Why did this man make her feel insecure about everything? With him near her, she couldn't be sure if what she saw and felt were her imagination or reality.

With Philip, she knew his intention and how he made her feel. She hadn't imagined the way he disliked her flaws or the disgust in his eyes. With Jarzell, she wasn't sure what he was thinking.

Would he show her his thoughts? They stood staring at each other, and heat traveled around her body. The air thickened in the room, and a woodsy smell entered her nose and calmed her nerves.

What was he thinking right now? Energy hummed between Rita and Jarzell, pulling them together.

A clearing of the throat sounded, but neither Jarzell nor Rita acknowledged it. A self-assured grin stretched across his face as if he just discovered something satisfying.

Lerma cleared her throat louder this time. Rita and Jarzell whipped their attention to her. Lerma offered an awkward smile. "I've got to help Valda with the books in the back. Rita will let you know which windowpanes need repairing."

"Thanks, Lerma." Rita snapped out of the trance-like state that held her to Jarzell. She released a breath, and he did too. Neither made a comment about what had just occurred.

"How are you today?" he asked, still looking at her like he was reading a story from her face.

"Okay, I guess. And you?"

His eyes narrowed. "Could be better."

"Oh, did something happen last night?" She remembered his meeting with Arkon. Had he discovered valuable information about the Ulkrins?

He stepped closer to her, and heat radiated from him. The desire in his gaze tingled her skin. "You came into my dream last night. I didn't like it."

What the hell?

SIX

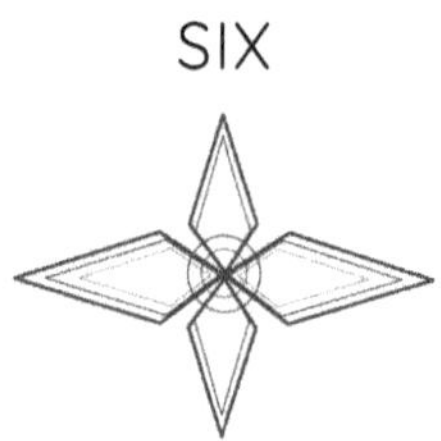

RITA STARED at him in disbelief. For a moment, she thought about Philip and wondered if all the male species had messed-up DNA in them. Or was she just doomed?

How was she supposed to reply to that? He didn't look angry, but his tone carried an edge she didn't like; an edge that reminded her too much of Philip.

She squared her shoulders, ready for battle. "I have no control over *your* dreams. It's not my fault—"

"Flekken." He let out a heavy sigh. "Sorry, that came out wrong. I'm not blaming you for anything. It's definitely not your fault. Let's just say it shocked me to dream about you."

He dreamed about her? She liked that idea more than she thought.

Rita pursed her lips. "Am I that atrocious that you'd be shocked to dream about me?" She meant that as a joke, but his serious expression remained. Unlike his confident self from yesterday, he appeared nervous. What had happened overnight?

"No, you're not. You're the most stunning female I've ever seen. The dream was so real. The emotion so raw, I didn't know what to do about it."

Talk about shock. This is beyond strange.

He scratched his head. "Do you have a minute to talk? I can start the window replacement right after."

"Yeah, sure. Come this way." She led him to her office and closed the door. "Do you want anything to drink?"

Gray eyes bore into her. "No thanks. I don't know how to explain this. I guess I'll start by saying that I saw an image of you floating in front of me a few days after I helped rescue you and your sisters. But then the image never came back, and I thought it was just my imagination." He swallowed, and his Adam's apple bobbed against the green skin.

What kind of image did she appear as? Was it translucent or did she appear like a tangible person? She didn't want to interrupt his explanation, so she let him continue.

"I've wanted to meet you, get to know you from the beginning, but I was sent away on business. I had to wait for the perfect time to come back and introduce myself without appearing strange." He paused and tucked his hands inside his pant pockets. "Then a week ago, your face reappeared in front of me in mist form again. You looked at me like you were waiting for me. I knew I had to come see you. As fate would have it, the case for the missing tablet flashed on the government's urgent list, and I grabbed it."

Rita had no words to reply. He'd been thinking about her all this time? Heat burst like little fireworks inside her, confirming that this odd rise in temperature she'd been feeling lately was connected to Jarzell somehow.

She'd been sketching him, and he'd been seeing her in mist form. Were they connecting to each other all this time in invisible ways?

"What did I do in your dream?" she asked.

"You were with another male." His jaw tightened as he

reached out a hand and brushed across her cheek. "I didn't like it." His voice was subtle and serious.

Rita's heart rate increased with his touch. What was the connection here? She'd dreamed of him too, and she also didn't like the idea of him with other females. What did this coincidence mean?

"I... I dreamed of you last night too."

His eyes sparked with hope. "I hope it was better than my dream."

"You were with an attractive female." Rita pressed her lips into a thin line. "And I didn't like that either."

He rocked back on his heels. "I enjoy hearing that." Then a crease formed between his eyebrows. "I wonder if our meeting has to do with a Saedo lore. There was a story about dreams and mist, but I'm not an expert on those things. But I know who is."

"Grandma Ova." This wise star-being was like a priestess. She knew things that others didn't.

He nodded. "We can pay her a visit. Maybe tomorrow? If you're available."

"I'd like that," she said. Would he mind if she assisted him to find the Sacred Tablet for the Village Library? She wasn't sure what the rules were with Chief Mozar. "Is it okay if I help you locate the tablet? It disappeared under my nose. I think I have a responsibility to find it."

"Maybe this is why we're coming together now."

Yes, she thought about that too.

"I'd love for you to help me." The tension on his face relaxed. "I woke up agitated, but now, I'm feeling a lot better."

"Me too."

He had no idea how irritated she'd been before he showed up. That would probably add an unnecessary layer to the beaming ego radiating from him.

Today had been another odd day, indeed. But it was a

pleasant change from yesterday. She just discovered the man she'd been secretly admiring also admired her back.

Though the heat in her body had subsided a little, it still lingered, like it was monitoring the two of them.

"Let's replace these windows. I don't want you in any danger." He checked his wristband and tapped something. "The droids will roll the panels in now."

It had been a long time since a man had shown genuine concern for her. She thought she had forgotten what that felt like, but Jarzell just reminded her how a woman should be treasured.

Something powerful brewed inside her. She prayed it would be something that kept her heart together. Things were moving faster than she expected, and she had a feeling they wouldn't slow down anytime soon. From her observation, he wasn't the type to slow down.

For Rita, she had to be careful. She couldn't afford to run without knowing where she was running to. She could very well run into a dead end and injure herself again. Baby steps proved to be safer. She had a mended heart and new lifestyle to protect now.

With that caution in mind, she said, "I sealed the cracked glass with a temporary bandage until someone could come fix it permanently, so if you need my assistance, I can help you."

He whirled to her, pride beaming on his face. "*You* did that? I was wondering who sealed it with great care. The glass-fuser isn't an easy device to use. I know a few males who are clumsy with it."

"I can do whatever job I put my mind to. I needed the job done, and there was no one around, so I did it."

"You did an admirable job."

Rita would be lying if she thought his approval didn't boost her self-confidence. "I used a soldering gun when I was on

Earth. The glass-fuser is more advanced, and the melted glass doesn't even give off a toxic smell. I have a knack for handiwork."

"I'm good with my hands too." He held up his large, green palms. "I can teach you whatever you want to learn."

Was that a flirt with a hidden agenda? An invitation for something more?

A smirk slid onto his lips as his eyes scanned her face.

Oh, yes, it is.

"How many have learned from your hands?" she asked, holding his gaze.

"You'll be the first. I've never made this offer before."

Jarzell reeled her in like a delighted fish on a hook. He didn't know how creative she preferred her men in bed. After all, she was an artist, so anything that expanded her imagination got brownie points. Though the innuendo could mean anything, she imagined him "teaching" her by showing her his handiwork. Her eyes wandered down to his masculine hand and fingers. Her core tightened as she envisioned his hands and fingers admiring her like a precious artwork.

Jarzell grinned, probably wondering what was going on in her mind. Embarrassment burned her cheeks, and she opened her office door, leading him down the hallway to the windows that needed replacing. In all the years she'd dated, no man had ever made her wet her panties from a damn smirk.

Rita was in deep trouble.

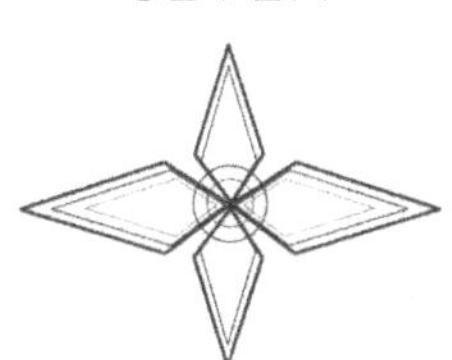

With the help of two droids, Jarzell didn't need Rita's assistance. She returned to her office and updated the task calendar for next month, placed supply orders, and reviewed upcoming projects. She wanted to cross off as many projects as possible, so her plate wouldn't be full when she returned from vacation. There were certain things that stayed the same no matter what planet she lived on. Responsibilities, work ethic, and time management didn't change in Saedo. If anything, she worked even harder here because she was grateful for the opportunity to start a brand-new life.

Rita looked forward to her time away from work. She needed to figure out the significance of this internal heat that resonated with Jarzell. Moreover, she felt called upon to search for the Sacred Tablet. On top of everything, her desire for Jarzell had increased the more time she spent with him. Was he part of the "new beginning" she needed? Knowing he felt the same way escalated their relationship.

Did they have a relationship yet? Not really.

What they had was an admission of attraction. She didn't need to wonder or assume about his feelings for her. He dreamed about her and admitted jealousy for something that had occurred in a dream. She'd reacted the same way to her dream of him. What was the connection here? It was like they had both entered a dream realm and emerged with their version of a story with a common theme: they didn't like seeing each other with someone else.

"What are you smiling about?" Jarzell's energy warmed her office space and disrupted her work.

Was she smiling?

"I'm just looking forward to some time off from work, that's all." That wasn't a lie. It was part of the truth.

"When are you taking time off?"

"Starting tomorrow."

Jarzell checked his wristband and pulled up a calendar, moving things around. "I've delegated two conference meetings and building infrastructure reviews to other team members. I can meet you tomorrow. We can visit Grandma Ova and then work on the case. What time works for you?"

Goodness, he was efficient. His mind worked fast. In addition to the tangible calendar on his wristband, he probably had a scheduler in his head too. Though a part of her found his efficiency and clarity sexy, a jolt of anxiety shot through her from his busy energy.

He seemed so fearless and confident. Could she keep up with his expectations? She was still piecing herself together. What if she didn't measure up to the woman he thought she was? Philip had made sure she knew about his disappointment of her. She didn't want to place that kind of pressure on herself again. If she worked hard at anything now, it would be for her inner growth and not some man's approval.

Rita kept that caution in the back of her mind as she gave herself a chance with Jarzell. "You can stop by around ten in the morning?" She wasn't a morning person, so she appreciated a few hours to lounge around.

"Sounds good." His thumb jerked behind him. "Your windows are all set. I'm taking the droids back to the center so others can use them. What time do you get out today? Have you been to The Crystalline SiSTARS café? It's a new café started by one of Saedo's citizens."

Her curiosity piqued. She'd heard Valda and Lerma talk about the popular hangout that offered amazing drinks and snacks. "I'd love to go. I can get out around five today."

"Great. Do you want me to pick you up?"

Excitement churned in her stomach. "Is this a date?"

"It sure is." He braced his hands on her desk, leaning over.

The scent of sweat, male, and something uniquely Jarzell snuck into her nose, making her want to take a deep inhale. "You move fast," she said.

"I want to make sure my dream is only a dream. I want others to know you're with me." A spark flickered in his eyes. "Why should we pretend things are something else when we're both attracted to each other? I don't like to play games."

Rita's heart pounded from the intensity of his gaze. "Neither do I."

"Excellent. I'd like to pick you up from your home, if that's okay."

The man had a concrete plan in his head. The pace at which his mind worked fascinated her. His words and actions flowed with confidence. Had anyone ever tripped him up before? Did his mind ever slow down?

She wanted to find out. Could she *affect* him in a way that surprised him? She'd have to wait and see.

EIGHT

JARZELL PICKED Rita up in a blue sports rider that glided gracefully on the road. It looked like a sports car on Earth, but with slick metal wings that could elevate them better than her personal rider, which was an adorable black coupe that ran on solar energy. The technology on her rider collected massive amounts of solar energy from the two suns, so she never had to worry about gas or mileage.

She reviewed the blinking monitor below his dashboard. "What's that?"

"It's a frequency reading for Saedo. After the past storm, the energies have shifted. We're monitoring them so we can prepare for any abrupt changes."

He pulled into the parking lot and got out. She yanked on her door handle, but it was still locked. He rounded the hood, pressed something on the car exterior, and her door slid open.

He offered her his hand. "Please allow me to escort you." A wide grin stretched on his face, and her heart jumped. "Isn't this what human females like in a man? I've studied Earthlings for a while."

"Do all star-beings study humans?" Rita smiled and placed

her small hand on his large palm. She didn't know what to expect on her first date with a star-being, but it wasn't this. Philip used to open the car door for her, but after a month, he stopped.

"We study what fascinates us." He squeezed her hand gently.

Would Jarzell soon stop this sweet gesture too? Even though she didn't need this kind of treatment, she welcomed it now and then. It was nice to see a man put in the extra effort to show his significant other that he cared.

"We do like it. You'd win a lot of hearts from showing respect to women." Heat blossomed at their joined hands.

"Am I winning yours? Your corra is the only one that interests me."

A corra was the star-beings' term for "heart." Jarzell was aiming straight for his target. He didn't beat around the bush, and she appreciated the honesty. But it would take her time to trust a man again.

Still, the no-nonsense question took her by surprise, and she didn't have an answer for him. She had a lot of feelings to sort through, and this recent attraction to him was something she needed to review and take her time understanding. She didn't want to admit to anything before she knew for certain that her heart was indeed shifting to him. She'd always favored long term relationships over fun times, but what about him?

How could Jarzell ask something like that when things had only started? Was he that certain of them? Or was this part of his confident character to move swiftly? Did he move from one female to another with swiftness too? These questions bombarded her, cautioning her.

He swung their hands like delightful teenagers. "You don't need to answer me right now. But I want to know when you have one."

"How many miles per hour up there?"

A crease dug into his forehead. "What do you mean?"

Rita tapped his temple. "Your mind works at a speed that's abnormal. I can't keep up with you."

Jarzell laughed, and the sound cheered up the street. "Abnormal makes things interesting. That's how I am. I can see and connect things in my head quickly. A lot of times, it drives people crazy. I have to remember that others need more time than me."

"Your brain is an overclocked processor. Isn't it tired of working too fast?"

Jarzell cocked his head. "Do you know that overclocking is when you trick a processor to run faster than it was meant to safely? Do you know a lot about computers?"

"Not really. I only heard the term overclocking from my ex-boyfriend. He was a computer engineer."

Jarzell nodded slowly, and Rita could imagine the wheels turning, probably debating whether to ask her to elaborate on Philip. She had no desire to have Philip intrude on her date.

"My brain works swiftly. But right now, I've given it a rest. I don't want my time with you to go fast. I want to savor every moment."

With that, her heart melted. She'd never been showered with such tender and honest words before. A part of her felt like they were too good to be true. But a deeper part yearned for this kind of attention. It had been too long since she felt cherished and special.

They strode by the StoryArt Gallery. Rita sighed, stopped, and stared at the new painting on display. The use of color mesmerized her. It sparkled, and the way it moved made her feel like she was entering a cosmic portal into another world. That was the power of art. Art could transport you to unimaginable places.

"You like art?" Jarzell asked.

"I do. I *love* it. I've always wanted to showcase my paintings in a gallery. Never had the guts to submit my work, though." Rita turned away from the display, and they continued walking to the café.

"Why not?" Jarzell asked.

Rita shrugged. "Never thought I was good enough." It surprised her that she could share that private part of her with him without hesitation.

"I think you're fabulous."

She laughed and blushed. "You haven't even seen any of my work." Would he want to see them? How would he react to her sketches of him?

"I'm certain your art is a reflection of you. Art reflects the artist, am I right? Since you're the most stunning female I've ever encountered, it would make sense your creations would be stunning too." He winked at her and brought on a whole new sexiness to winking. "I'd like to see your art sometime."

Her heart thudded. "Okay."

Jarzell and Rita entered The Crystalline SiSTARS Café. They took a tray and walked around various booths where an assortment of food came out on a conveyor belt for them to choose. Rita glanced into the open kitchen where droids and star-beings prepared the food. She liked the idea of seeing what happened in the kitchen.

Vanessa's restaurant should be ready to open in a month. Had Vanessa stopped by to check out her competition? This café had a different flair than her sister's style, and the food was more like a variety of appetizers, whereas Vanessa's menu had a lot of human dishes with an alien twist.

Rita used a tong and grabbed two Chanterelle mushrooms that smelled fruity. The label read "for strong hair and nails." She could use that in her diet. Most of the food in Saedo aided in health and vitality. After filling their plates with an abundance of delicacies, they found a table by the corner.

A female star-being with wild hair made of tentacles strode up to their table. One tentacle held the tablet while she clasped her hands together and grinned at Rita and Jarzell. "What would you like to drink?" She splashed a large virtual screen with vast selections of drinks, all of which consisted of some type of crystal.

Rita chose the fruit shake with amazonite glitter and Jarzell ordered the cosmic float with amethyst chunks. She didn't know she could ingest crystals. Rock sugar and granules of salt were the only "crystal-like" things she'd eaten.

After the waitress left, she asked, "Is it safe to eat these crystals?"

"Yes, that's the café's specialty. They process crystals in a way that makes them edible and beneficial to your body. The café is owned by a group of female star-beings from Celeron and Terrakado. Tammo's sister, Kress, is one of the founders." He glanced around, searching for her. "I don't see her around right now."

She vaguely remembered meeting Tammo at one of Inga's fashion show. He was another soldier.

Jarzell jerked his chin toward the workers. "As you can see, the wait staff comprises of all kinds of beings from various provinces and planets."

Rita noticed the various skin tones, textures, tails, and tentacles on the star-beings.

"Do you have a favorite café back on Earth?" he asked.

Rita thought about all the abundant coffee shops she visited, but only one stood out to her. "I like going to this small shop in my city. The couple who owns it fell in love while he managed the shop, and she was a repeat customer. They bought the shop when the previous owners decided to close it. It's a cute place, but it doesn't offer anything close to what this innovative shop offers. Have you been to Earth?"

"A few times, not as many as I'd like to. My brother, Huelik, gets to travel to the Milky Way and Earth more often. He's a soldier and part of a team that travels to that area."

Maybe she could visit Earth with Jarzell when the time came. She swerved her mind back to the unique shop she sat in. The name of the café fascinated her. "What does 'SiSTARS' mean? Is it like a different way of saying and spelling sisters?"

He nodded. "Sort of. 'Sistar' is a term used to address a female friend. It's like acknowledging the sacred bond or friendship between females who support each other. And because star-beings live amongst the stars, that's a suitable description for the female entourage. For us males, we are just brothers."

That was an interesting take on friendships between women. Rita was lucky to have blood sisters who loved and supported her. But she'd known women who didn't get along with theirs and found support from the people around them. Female friends were truly special. She looked around, hoping to get a glimpse of the "sistars," but she didn't see any star-beings that stood out.

Behind her was a table with three attractive female-star beings. The gorgeous star-being with yellow hair stared at Jarzell, but so did a lot of females in the café.

"I'll never look at a crystal the same way again." Rita examined the table she was at and the chair she sat on. They were made from clusters of crystals, making it appear like she was sitting on some cosmic furniture.

Jarzell smiled. "Humans use crystals too. They just don't know the crystals' capabilities. Crystals are in your computers, in all your electronic devices. Humans use a lot of quartz crystals. They have a unique ability to convert electrical energy into mechanical energy through an effect called piezoelectricity." He gestured his hands toward the outside. "There are treasures in the lands, even on Earth. If you love and take care of the land, it will take care of you back."

Rita thought about that for a bit. From her experience on Earth, few people believed in taking care of the planet. But here in Saedo, she'd witnessed how these star-beings cherished their land. The advancement in technology, including the plants that provided food, had healing properties that were beyond her imagination. Was that an example of the land blessing its inhabitants?

Her mind hopped to a different topic. "Is this why the Ulkrins want Saedo? For its treasures?"

"That's one reason; the other reason is power. As far as I know, the desire for power has corrupted civilizations from all the galaxies."

Rita thought about Earth and couldn't agree more. From what she saw on the news and read in books, she understood why peace was difficult to attain. Countries wanted power and gaining land meant resources, and resources became power. It was a never-ending cycle that boggled her mind. Star-beings weren't that different from humans after all.

Jarzell popped a squishy ball sprinkled with crystals into his mouth, chewed, and swallowed. "Agarrek is filled with darkness, violence, and greed. The Ulkrins took over that province several solar-cycles ago, and they've allowed other star races who share their beliefs to live there. The true Agarrek citizens don't have the power or army to fight the Ulkrins."

"Did you discover something about the squirmurs that could help beat the Ulkrins?"

Jarzell leaned in and whispered, probably not wanting to share details with the public. "Yes, we believe there's a way to infiltrate Agarrek. But that's going to take some time for our engineers to work through and test."

Rita appreciated his trust in her. He didn't have to tell her anything, but he chose to share it. She remembered a time when trust was something she never had to worry about. That feeling was slowly blooming in her again.

At that thought, teal mist emerged from his shoulders and arms. This was the same color mist that had come from her sketch of him. She hadn't been hallucinating.

A sensation she didn't understand stirred in her. She knew what seeing the mist meant. She'd had discussions about it with her sisters. Now that she could see it, she didn't know what to think, or how to react. It was like fate handing her something she wasn't ready for. What should she do with this information?

Her attraction to him was one thing, but now this elevated their relationship even more.

Jarzell sipped his cosmic float and stared at her. "Are you okay?"

Rita debated on whether to tell him or not? She decided to wait another day. She needed her emotions to settle and solidify. Right now, she stood on unstable ground. She just wanted to enjoy her first date and not think about the complexity of it.

"Just trying to remember everything about my first date in Saedo." She sipped her fruit shake, and the sweetness of the crystal glitter sizzled on her tongue. "And my first-time eating amethyst crystals."

He nodded, but he could tell she wasn't giving him the whole truth.

While they ate and drank, they carried on a casual conversation that flowed with ease. She felt like she'd known him for a long time. Was this the familiar feeling of someone she connected with? It was hard to tell.

His wristband buzzed. He glanced at it but ignored the message. He stared at her—or was he looking past her? Rita turned around and only saw the group of attractive female star-beings.

She whirled back. "Is something wrong?"

"No, just appreciating my companion for the evening. You have my full attention." A smile slid onto his lips.

Damn it. He was keeping something from her, just like how she kept the mist from him.

They stared at each other for a moment, and a mutual understanding passed between them. The moment pulsed and stretched until it snapped with laughter.

"Let's be honest here. We both have something to share, but tonight isn't that time. Agree?"

"Agreed," Rita said, glancing at her smart bracelet. It was nine at night. She'd been chatting with him for three hours. It seemed like they just sat down.

"You have a tiny amethyst crystal right here." He leaned in, and his tongue licked the corner of her lips. A thrill shot down her spine.

He sat back in his chair and studied her reaction to him. His gaze slid from her lips to her eyes. Heat increased in her body, as pleasure spread through her core, forcing her lips to part.

But she had no comment. What could she say?

She liked his bold gesture. She liked that he took what he wanted. That courage and confidence inspired her to take what she wanted too. He didn't know how bold she could be. The self-assured grin on his lips encouraged her to show him.

Normally, Rita wouldn't do something like this. But there was nothing "normal" about her having a date with a handsome green star-being on an undiscovered planet. There was nothing typical about her powerful attraction to him way before this date. She had a sketchbook full of drawings of him. Was that normal? Absolutely not. Did she care? Nope.

Right now, she didn't give a damn about anything. All she wanted was to show this man who he was dating.

With a serious expression, she crooked a finger at him. "Come here."

Intrigue glistened in his eyes as he leaned forward.

"Let me feed you." With her tongue, she scooped some amethyst crystals from her shake and showed him her intention.

When he gasped, his mouth opened, and her tongue slid in, feeding him more sweet crystals. He let out a low moan. Chatter faded into the background. She didn't know if anyone was watching them, but she didn't care. They kissed, tasting each other playfully. Oh, yes, his tongue had skills and knew how to play, sliding under and over hers. His hand went around her neck, pulling her closer, and he deepened the kiss.

The musky scent of him seduced her, making her want him right there in the café.

She placed a gentle hand on his face and pulled away. Her emotions and her body wanted him and blocked out all logic. She reminded herself about pacing and caution.

"I don't want to give the public a show." Rita looked into gray eyes that had darkened significantly. "Besides, we should slow down so we don't hit a wall without knowing."

The boldness shocked and elated her. She feared what he could inspire her to do next.

Jarzell ran a hand through his brown hair that glinted bronze in the light and stared at her. "You make me feel so much, and I can't seem to control myself. But I'll try. The last thing I want to do is to scare you away."

"I want to see where this relationship is going too. I want to ensure it lasts, and that can only happen when I can think clearly. I feel a lot too." She switched the topic to lighten the situation. "You're bold for a first date." That statement could be applied to her too.

He shrugged. "I see what I like, and I go for it. Why wait and waste time? I like how my body reacts to you, and how you react to me. We have perfect chemistry." He flicked her a gaze full of promise. "The next time we kiss, it won't be quick." He licked his lips. "I love the way you taste, and I want to explore what other flavors you have."

This man could make her lose her breath and brain all at once. "Is this how you act on every first date?"

"No, just with you."

Sexual energy sizzled between them.

"When was your last relationship?" Rita asked.

"My serious relationship ended two solar-cycles ago. The last time I was with a female was six months ago."

She didn't think a face like his would remain single for long. She'd already counted five female star-beings who had snuck him an admiring look while they were getting their food. He didn't notice them, but she did. She wanted to know what had happened to his serious relationship, but she wasn't ready to open that can of worms yet. She didn't want to talk about her ex-boyfriend either.

Jarzell grinned and the light in the café made his green skin glisten like he was made of crystals. "This has been the best date I've ever had. Let's finish dinner, so we can call it a night. I want you well rested for tomorrow. I have a busy day of investigation planned for us. There's a place that might give us a clue about the missing tablet."

NINE

Rita woke before the suns came up and brought in the food Emma had sent a droid to deliver to her doorstep. Rita placed the food into the coldbox and made herself a mug of herbal tea Vanessa had given her to try. The floral fragrance soothed her stomach. She sensed the heat more today. It circulated around her body, making her fully aware of its presence. Why was she feeling this odd heat?

Last night, she had gone to bed thinking about Jarzell and his mist.

Something changed in her. The unknown frightened and excited her at the same time. Jarzell was part of this excitement, but could he also be the fear? She admired and appreciated his efficiency, and the clarity in which he saw things and went after them. She knew many men who were unsure of themselves. Confidence carved an easier path for everyone. However, a part of her wondered if his efficiency, his impatience, would create a wedge between them.

Rita wasn't impatient. She could be for certain things, but most times, she preferred to take things slowly. There was a natural cycle to things. Even when she created art, she needed time for ideas and colors to sink in. She couldn't rush the process. The times when she did, she ended up hating what she produced.

She huffed out a breath as she realized why she was bothered by this insecurity. Jarzell had one thing in common with Philip. They were both impatient. In the beginning of her relationship with Philip, she'd accepted his urgent ways, thinking she could inspire him to slow down. That never worked out. His attitude toward her became cruel, like he had no time and patience for her.

And though Jarzell displayed impatience and wanted things done swiftly, she felt it was different with him. Could she trust herself with that judgment? When she was attracted to someone, she saw them in a different light, and that light could hide ugly shadows.

Rita didn't want to experience that pain and shame again. She was healing now. She didn't want to fall back into that dark hole. Who knew if she could crawl back out this time?

The wish she had tossed out to the Universe on that fateful New Year's Eve night came back into her mind.

I deserve a man who loves me for my wounds and for all I aspire to be.

All her sisters had made a wish that night as well. They came true for Emma, Sasha, Inga, and Vanessa. Was Jarzell that man for her? She was afraid to expect anything. Expectations sometimes backfired. A headache pounded at her temples.

Not wanting to think about the topic anymore, she poured more hot water into her mug and stared through the window at where the two suns broke the horizon. What did Jarzell have planned for today?

Rita was about to sip her tea when teal mist formed an image of Jarzell's face above the mug. She gasped, dropped the mug on the counter, and jumped back from reflex. She grabbed some towels and cleaned up the spilled tea. Luckily, the mug didn't break.

The abstract image of Jarzell wasn't frightening or anything. The mist moved in slow motion, making the face appear as if it was looking at her, trying to converse with her.

A thrill skated down her back, and she had a feeling that the teal mist symbolized more than a simple starmate connection.

Rita spent a couple of hours researching Saedo lore through the Galacto Net. Some lore spoke of events in the land that foreshadowed big changes were about to occur. Other lore suggested that ancestors were watching over the land, guiding certain individuals to assist in protecting the land. She recognized the lore about the blooming of blessiums, which were rare flowers that budded after connecting starmates.

She had heard all about this from her sisters. How Emma, Sasha, Inga, and Vanessa all found their starmates by recognizing the color of their lover's mist. Each soldier gave off a specific color mist that no one else could see but their starmate, their forever mate. Not only that, their love for each other inspired a blessium to bud that matched the mist's color.

Emma was yellow; Sasha was blue; Inga was red; and Vanessa had a purple flower. The mystery of the Universe was something no one could understand. Grandma Ova told them that each flower represented a color on the love spectrum—a cosmic frequency that nourished the land and everything around it.

Saedo thrived because more love vibrated in its land. But with the increase in fertile energy and land, that also attracted enemies who wanted power over it.

Rita searched the Galacto Net for information on undetected body temperature for humans on different planets, but found nothing that resonated or made any sense.

She hoped Grandma Ova could answer some questions for her. Her smart bracelet buzzed with a message from Jarzell.

Be there soon. Got you coffee and breakfast.

He added an adorable animation of him offering an adorable version of her a plate of sparkling something. She liked this new aspect of him; the playful side that showed he could take things lightly, that he wasn't always serious.

You didn't have to, but thanks! She only added a smiley face because she couldn't find that animation section. Maybe she didn't have it available on her smart bracelet. It was already nine o'clock. She'd spent the early morning researching and her stomach hadn't even growled. Maybe it had, but she didn't notice. On a normal day, she would've had coffee and a breakfast muffin already. But her routine was different today.

Everything had become different recently. She was a chameleon, so adapting to change wasn't hard.

Rita turned off her computer and rushed into the bedroom. Holy shit, she was a mess. Her hair resembled a purple bird's nest. She threw on knit capris made from materials that increased metabolism in her body and tightened her buttocks, thighs, and calves every time she moved.

A knock sounded at her door.

"Already?" She'd only received his message two minutes ago.

Rita strode to the door and opened it. He stepped in, closing the door behind him. His eyes raked across her face and down her body.

A wide smile formed on his lips as he strode to her kitchen counter, placing down the cup of coffee and a bag of treats. "Did you just wake up? Did I rush you?"

"No, I've been up. I was researching when you sent me a message. I lost track of time." Rita's hand went to her messy bun and was about to unravel it.

"No, let me." He gripped her wrist and drew her hand down. "I like this disheveled look on you. It makes me want to get messy with you." His voice was soft, with enough roughness that aroused her.

Rita was definitely off-kilter if she could be stirred this easily. Did he have some secret remote control? Sexual heat and slickness pooled at her thighs. Now, she had to change her panties too.

"Do you want to get messy with me, Rita?" The green of his skin darkened. Were her eyes playing tricks on her? No, the color of his skin fluctuated in various shades of green, making him appear like a moving palette of color, mesmerizing her.

The word "messy" took on a whole new meaning for Rita. A slew of sexy ideas popped into her mind. She wanted to make messy art with him, rolling naked all covered in paint. She wanted to teach him patience, and if he learned it, he'd be rewarded with sloppy kisses, dirty words, and...

Oh, God. Where was her self-control? Where was her logical mind?

Rita reeled in her imagination, because it was the only way she and Jarzell would leave her apartment clothed to get things done. But goodness, her body wanted to know his idea of "messy."

"Yes." Her eyes drilled into his. "But not right now. We have things to do."

A crooked smile crawled onto his lips, creating the perfect image for a sketch.

"Excellent." He turned to the coffee. "You should eat something before we go. I got you four pastries." He opened the bag and took out two floral muffins topped with edible dried flowers. One was purple, the other a pale pink. She'd never had a Danish covered with tiny aquamarine crystals. The stylish croissant with sweet pink berries was one of her favorites.

"Always thinking ahead, huh? That's a lot of pastries for just me. You should have some."

"They're all yours. I wasn't sure what you liked, so I got a variety. It's better to have more than enough than not enough. Save some for tomorrow. They'll keep for a few days in the coldbox."

After Rita changed into a lilac blouse and brushed her hair, she ate the croissant and sipped the Saedo coffee, one of the best coffees she'd ever had.

"Where are we going today?" She asked while he strode around her living room. *Crap.* She rose from her seat. "I'm such a terrible host. I forgot to give you a tour. This is my home, and you're in my living room."

He whirled and smiled. "I can give myself a tour. You can take your time with your breakfast. Where's your art? I want to see it."

He remembers. Not that she didn't want to display her art in her own home. She hadn't been motivated to create art until now. Her sketchbook was sandwiched between other books on her bookcase. Was she ready to show him her sketches? Sharing an abstract or landscape art was different from revealing her illustrations of his face. That was too private for now.

"I had a lot of art back on Earth. I stopped painting for a while, but recently, I've been inspired."

"Oh." Disappointment tugged on his face. He strode over and sat down beside her. "Why did you stop painting?"

This was the dreaded question. It was like he saw the bandage and wanted to know the wound it covered. She couldn't give him a simple answer and be done with it. The way he looked at her showed a curious man who wanted all the details.

Was she ready to share them? Would Jarzell think she had no spine for crumbling because of a man's rejection? Did she care about his opinion? To a point, yes, but she was done with what men thought of her. If Jarzell didn't like what he heard, then he could leave.

Rita inhaled a deep breath, straightening her back. "I got into a car accident a little over a year ago, and the car caught on fire. I was burned quite badly on my back. It left scars that go up to the back of my neck." She met his eyes, giving him the answers he never got in the beginning. "That's why I often wear my hair down."

"I like your hair up and down." His gaze never left hers. "That experience must have been traumatic."

"It was. I feared heat and fire for a while. But I'm better now." Feeling more relaxed, she crossed her legs. "Anyway, that's just part of why I stopped making art. I had a boyfriend, Philip. After the accident, he saw me as a damaged person, but I think his perception had always been that way. I just didn't realize it until it was too late. He didn't like the scars on my back and made sure I knew it. I came home one day and found him with a friend of mine."

"What?" Jarzell reached for her hand like he knew the memory stabbed at her again.

"That betrayal cut me deeply," Rita said. "When you're feeling flawed and unworthy, you crawl into a dark corner where you can't see yourself or anything else. The pitch black became my haven. I quit my job as a high school art teacher. I just didn't have the energy to dedicate to the kids. I had enough money saved up, so I took a part-time job while I figured out what to do. I fell into a deep depression."

With his jaw set and eyes sharp like blades, he said, "He deserves a torturous death for putting you through hell. Where is he now?"

Rita hadn't seen this dangerous look on Jarzell before. His

voice carried a stinging edge that could make someone bleed. Despite that, it warmed her heart that he cared.

"I don't know. He's probably with another woman. But I believe what goes around comes around. Philip doesn't bother me anymore. The tough part is trying to forgive myself for not being strong enough to see that he was wrong for me from the beginning. I *wasn't* the problem. I shouldn't have let him hurt me like that. I should've known better, you know?"

Jarzell brushed a hand down her cheek, and heat zipped through her. "We all have lessons to learn, and we all learn differently. What I see in front of me is a strong woman who recognizes her weakness. That, in itself, is a powerful attribute. I've known many males who have trouble facing their weaknesses because they think it makes them vulnerable. No one is perfect. I have areas that can be improved. I know that. Acknowledging a flaw is a strength, taking action to heal that flaw is an even stronger power."

His outlook revealed another aspect of him that made him more attractive. She'd always had a weakness for intelligent men. But he didn't need to know that right now. If he asked her what action she took to overcome that "weakness," how should she answer? The only answer she could give was tending to herself one day at a time.

"I didn't realize you were so wise," Rita said.

"It comes with living a long time. I'm two hundred and fifty-one solar cycles, and you're only twenty-seven years old."

She didn't bother asking how he knew that. He worked for the government, and they probably had all the information on her and her sisters when they became permanent residents of Saedo. She'd learned from her sisters that these star-beings aged differently because planet Celeron existed in an eighth-dimensional matrix, whereas Earth existed in a third-dimensional matrix. There was more density on Earth, and time was tricky when energies were involved. Though she didn't quite understand the science of it, she understood the concept on a different level. It was like art; some you couldn't describe, yet they were astounding to look at. You could appreciate them regardless of the questions they posed.

All of this deep talk opened her up to him. "I lost all desire and inspiration to create until..."

She took a moment to gather herself before she shared this secret with him.

His eyebrow arched. "Until..."

Her heart hammered, and her cheeks burned.

Inquisitiveness glittered in his eyes. "I *have* to know why you're blushing. It's sexy."

She blushed even more. She yanked her hand from his grip and covered her face with both hands, laughing. She had no idea why she was blushing, laughing, and feeling giddy and silly at the same time. What was wrong with her?

It was so out of character for her—wait a second—this sudden joy was how she used to be before the doom and gloom. This carefree state of pure creative energy where all her joyful emotions came about. It was back! Exhilaration rushed through her like a shooting star, giving her hope. She removed her hands from her face and looked at him.

He wore a curious grin that made him adorable. "I'd give anything for you to tell me what that was about? Are you laughing at me?"

She shook her head. "No, no. I wasn't laughing at you." An idea teased her. She recognized when a rare opportunity presented itself. It would be foolish to let it go. "Are you serious about that offer?"

"About what offer?"

"That you'd *give* anything to find out why my cheeks turned red?"

Jarzell considered her for a moment, probably not expecting her to take his statement seriously. There was a gem in that statement, and Rita found it.

"Of course," he said. "I keep my word. But I'm afraid to find out now." Amusement flickered in his eyes.

"I thought a soldier fears nothing."

"I don't fear what I can anticipate. But I'm afraid of how you can make me feel." His voice lowered. "This powerful attraction to you is new to me. I'm still trying to understand it. Also, you have a way of getting things from me that no other female has successfully done before. There's power in that, Rita."

The way he said her name was like a varnish on a painting that made it shinier and special.

She tossed him a warm smile. "I blushed because of you."

"Oh, yeah?" He scooted closer, and the skin on his face fluctuated again. She could see tiny veins under his skin as though the epidermis became transparent for a moment. "Tell me more."

"I don't have big artwork here to hang on my wall, but I have a sketchbook with sketches... of you."

Confusion, bafflement, and delight took their time on his stunning face, showing her the various emotions in him. "You do?"

She nodded, and his face beamed like a refined gem.

"When I first saw you, my eyes snapped an image of you in my head. You were the first star-being my eyes caught and remembered. I was captivated. You have such fine features." Her fingers traced his jawline. "So, I started sketching. One sketch led to another, and before I knew it, I had a collection of you."

"Wow. I did not expect that at all." His eyes held hers. "I *inspired* you to create again?"

Rita gently pinched his cheek in a playful manner. "You did. You're my muse."

"That's the best compliment I've ever gotten. And your ex-boyfriend was a loser who didn't know what he had. You weren't meant for him. You're meant for *me*," Jarzell said that with so much certainty Rita had to look away to calm her racing heart. His declaration was like an artistic signature that marked her to him, and vice versa.

How could he be so sure about them? He didn't even know that she could see his teal mist. But did that matter to him? Right now, it didn't seem like he cared about that kind of Saedo lore.

"Were you ever going to tell me about your sketches if I hadn't stopped by the library and got the ball rolling between us?"

"I don't know." She shrugged. In her mind, their relationship had already started with the first sketch of him. "Art is an intimate relationship between the creator and his or her creation. A week ago, I wasn't ready to share my art with anyone, but now I'm ready to share it with you."

"Good, because I want to see what I look like through your eyes." His wristband buzzed, and a reminder popped up. "We should get going soon before the campground gets crowded. I'll take a raincheck on the sketchbook. That's one thing I want to take my time reviewing. Can I see it tonight?"

"Sure." There was one more thing she needed a raincheck on. "Would you give me two hours of your time to satisfy a creative idea?"

He didn't need to know the details yet. She was still exploring the various ways she wanted to be creative with him.

The other reason was wanting to use this opportunity to test his impatience. Could she teach him to slow his pace? How would he react?

He crossed his arms. "Whatever you want. I'll give you a full day of my time. What do you have planned for me, Creatress?"

No one had ever used that term to address her before. She liked it. On Earth, she was known as an artist. She didn't mind being a "Creatress" in Saedo.

"Let's just say it can get 'messy.'" Rita rose from her chair and put the rest of the pastries away.

"You can't just tease me with that. I need more."

Rita laughed on the inside, knowing she had tugged his impatient chord. *Let's see how far you can go before it snaps.*

He got up and followed her around the apartment as she closed her windows, preparing to go out. "You're torturing me on purpose."

Rita tossed him an innocent look. "Do I look like a woman who can hurt anyone?"

"You're a shrewd woman who just gained a day of my time without me fully knowing what I'm in for." He narrowed his eyes at her. "That makes you dangerous."

She laughed. "No one has ever described me as dangerous, but it's something I don't mind exploring with you. You'll benefit from this ordeal, I promise. It's nothing you have to worry about, plan, or need further details. You don't even need to put it on your calendar. We're going to be spontaneous. I'll let you know when the 'event' happens. Just relax and focus on your task for today."

He pursed his lips at her. "If we weren't crunched for time right now, I'd interrogate you until you give in."

"Well, then it's a good thing we have to find the Sacred

Tablet." Rita strode to the front door and slipped into her comfortable shoes. "Where are we going?"

"To the Derwood Creek. That was where my brothers and I fought off the squirmurs during the alien storm. I had a strange experience when I was there. I haven't told anyone about it. You'll be the first."

TEN

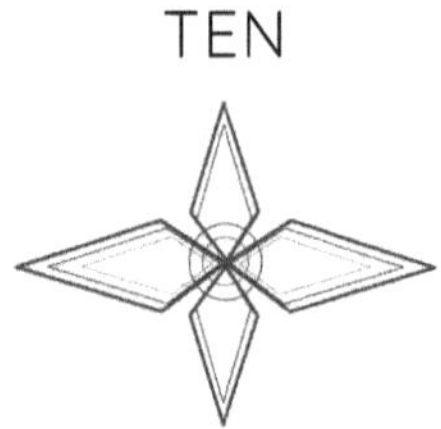

"What kind of strange experience?" Rita asked as she followed Jarzell down a dirt path, passing a massive stone carved with the universal words Derwood Creek Campground.

They strode by trees with enormous trunks and shrubberies full of fragrant flowers ranging from pinks, yellows, blues, to purples. The sweet fragrance from the abundant flowers welcomed her, nudging her forward. Birds chirped and chattered somewhere. An insect that looked like a purple bumblebee —twice the size of ones on Earth—buzzed around them and landed on Jarzell's shoulder.

"You have a giant bug on you." She pointed as it flapped its iridescent wings.

Jarzell swatted it away. "They're purple mellis, excellent pollinators. They're originally from the Province of Finntoro, which is just on the other side of this campground. These insects are similar to bees on Earth. These mellis make a tasty purple honey."

The mellis buzzed around Rita and flew toward a bush with yellow flowers.

The fresh air invigorated Rita's lungs as sounds of running

water became more melodic the deeper she immersed herself in the lush vegetation.

A loud flap of wings swooshed nearby. Jarzell nudged her behind him. A hand gripped the silver blaster on his waistband while he surveyed the area.

"No need to fear, my friend. It's just me." A beautiful man with a set of magnificent blue wings emerged from behind a wide tree trunk. He had midnight hair and sparkling sun-kissed skin. He wore a fitted dark top and leather pants that revealed a muscular body. He strode toward them. "It's been a long time, Jarzell. How are things?"

Jarzell released his grip on his blaster, released a sigh, stepping closer to Rita. She gawked at him, wondering if he was a star-being from a different province. She'd never seen such stunning blue wings before. Could he be a humanoid with bird aspects?

"Things are interesting in my realm," Jarzell said. "I'm sure they're more interesting in yours. What are you doing here?"

"Searching for someone. I picked up his scent in this dimension, but it appears he only passed by your planet." The man looked at her with potent blue eyes that glowed. Was he another star-being from a different province?

"Rita, this is my friend Daedriel."

Daedriel offered a warm smile, which she returned.

"We'll catch up another time," Daedriel said. "I've got to head to Earth. Nice meeting you, Rita." He expanded his gorgeous blue wings and took off into the sky.

She whipped a curious glance at Jarzell. "Is he an angel or some kind of bird-man?"

"A seraph from the twelfth-dimensional matrix. He helped us win a galactic battle a long time ago."

Encountering an angel on an alien planet was the last thing she expected. In her mind, they belonged in different worlds.

But then again, she belonged on Earth, and yet she stood on an undiscovered planet next to a star-being, one she had kissed not too long ago. She stared up at the blue sky expecting a dragon to surface, spitting out fire or something.

Angels came from the divine dimension, didn't they? So seeing one was like seeing a shooting star, right? If that was true, then Daedriel's sudden appearance could mean something important. Could this angel be a sign from the Universe telling her to keep an open mind; to expect the unexpected; to accept the fantastical things that often don't make sense? Or was his presence reminding her to keep the faith no matter what happened around her?

"The Universe continues to surprise me," Rita said as they continued on the dirt path.

"It's a vast place with complicated layers and portals. The Universe—or the Cosmos—is just one big home for all beings." Jarzell led her by several trees with interesting textures on their bark.

She took in the unique texture. She loved adding depths to her paintings, and interesting texture was one way to do that.

Jarzell came to a stop. "While we fought off the squirmurs, one of them flung itself at me. My body should have been slammed into the Saedo cedrus over there." He pointed to a tall tree that resembled a cedar on Earth, but with bluish leaves. "As I was in the air, an intangible force from the creek pulled me into it. I fell into the water. Oddly, the water felt like a blanket that cushioned my fall."

Jarzell offered his hand to assist her over a rock covered in pink moss. She took it and hopped across to stable ground filled with lush green grass.

"Maybe your ancestors were watching over you," Rita said.

It had taken her a while to believe that she had been protected during the car fire. It could've ended a lot worse. She could've died or been burned everywhere. Fortunately, she only acquired scars on her back, and those she could easily cover. Not that they mattered anymore.

Her scars didn't bother her any longer. The feeling of not being worthy or perfect was no longer prominent in her mind. Why was that? She'd think about that more when she had time alone.

"There's a lore that says nature speaks in subtle ways. I wonder if my body will react to the water here again." Jarzell took off his boots, rolled up his high-tech denim pants, and stepped into the water. Teal mist emerged from him and drifted above the water.

"Wow, that's beautiful," Rita said, waving at the vapors that snaked around her body.

He whirled, meeting her eyes. "You see my mist?"

She couldn't keep that fact from him now. He deserved to know the truth. Besides, she had a feeling the mist was trying to give her a clue anyway. "Yes, I see it. Your color is beautiful."

He didn't show the surprise she expected. His expression showed relief.

"I wondered if you'd be the one to see it." His eyes warmed on her. "I'm glad it's you. Come join me. The water is warm."

Rita rolled up her high-tech capris, kicked off her shoes, and joined him. The water currents moved around Jarzell and Rita like a greeting.

The teal mist increased in density, covering the creek in various shades of teal. The teal blended with a white fog she didn't notice before. They stayed in the creek for a little while, admiring the teal mist and white fog playing with each other.

Jarzell placed a hand to his ears. "I hear whispers."

"What do they say?" she asked.

"Just some ancient words. They weren't complete

sentences. Something about mist, smoke, water, fire, storytelling, and a few other words I didn't catch."

Revelation woke her like a splash of cold water. "The creek wanted us here."

Jarzell bent down and cupped water into his palms. "I agree."

She stepped out of the creek and put on her shoes, while he did the same with his boots.

Rita sniffed at an unfamiliar scent. "Do you smell that?"

He looked toward the giant tree. "It's the fragrance of the cedrus tree." He looked at her, and then past her at something.

"What are you looking at?" Rita asked.

"There's white smoke coming from your back."

"No way." Rita swiveled, and sure enough, streams of white smoke floated where she had stood. It weaved and connected with the mist, becoming an aqua color.

"This is weird." She sniffed again. "Am I giving off a burning smell?"

A subtle anxiety slithered inside her, but she doused it. Fire and heat didn't affect her like before.

Jarzell played with the smoke, waving his fingers through it, just as she had done with his mist. "It's a lovely aroma. There's a lore about this too, but I'm not familiar with it. I think it's time we stop by Grandma Ova's home for some answers."

She eyed her arms and hands, watching for the smoke to seep through her pores. Nothing happened. "The smoke isn't coming from anywhere else except my back. Why?"

"What do you have on your back?" His question came out in a way that appeared as though he already knew the answer and was guiding her to find out for herself.

Rita twisted her lips in a thinking manner. Revelation burst out of her. Could it really be her scars? She didn't feel discomfort or anything emitting from her back. The scars had been a part of her for so long it was as though they had always been there; a part that no longer bothered or shamed her.

Was the smoke a part of her healing? Had she reached an unknown milestone that had caused the smoke to emerge? Did the smoke symbolize the release of her mental chains?

Her healing journey took a positive turn when she landed in Saedo, or rather, when she began sketching Jarzell. With each sketch, she erased a little of her scars; a little of her trauma.

When she shared about her depression and shame with Jarzell, she lifted the bandage and released everything. She didn't even make that connection until now. Her body shivered as if the invisible cardigan fell off her body, taking all the fear and shame with it. She didn't need her cardigan to hide her scars anymore. She didn't care who saw them.

"My scars... is that possible? I mean, I see teal mist coming from you, but you're a star-being. I'm just a human. I don't think I've ever heard of a human giving off smoke unless it's meant metaphorically. But I'm not angry right now, so there shouldn't be any 'steam' coming from me."

He placed a hand on each of her shoulders. "Humans are special beings too. You have a lot of potential." He tapped her head. "You just haven't discovered all of your abilities yet. Don't forget that you're now living on a different planet with higher frequencies. Your body is 'open' to new things."

She remembered seeing his misty face rising up from her mug. Perhaps the mist and smoke had been trying to communicate with her all this time, and she was only acknowledging them now.

"Do you think this has something to do with the missing tablet?"

"I know it does, but I don't know why. We'll find out together."

Of all the places she could work at, she chose the Village

Library because she loved stories. She could have asked to work at the art gallery, but she didn't want the reminder of her past, of how she wasn't a good enough artist. An art gallery displayed perfect art, and at that time, she didn't feel "perfect" in any way. The safety of words and stories in books gave her an escape to heal without that reminder. The Universe knew what was best for her and placed her in the library for this healing purpose.

Words and art created stories in their own way, and she was the artist who could blend them both into one coherent story-line. Maybe this ability was how she could help this investigation.

This trip to Derwood Creek had opened some doors she'd never expected. A small part of her feared what lay beyond those doorways, but the curious part of her—the artist in her—urged her to continue. The unknown terrified people, including her. How many times had she let fear stop her from achieving something? There were too many to count. She recalled how fire used to induce panic in her, but no more.

Jarzell sat down on the grass and patted the spot beside him. "Derwood Creek is on the border of the Province of Finntoro. They've been our allies for a long time. With their help, we cleaned up this area after that battle with the squirmurs during the alien storm."

Beside him, Rita crisscrossed her legs. "Are the Ulkrins giving them a headache too?"

"Yes, but the Ulkrins are focused on Saedo. Finntoro has their own issues to deal with. If they need our help, we'll assist them just like how they assisted us." He pulled up a virtual screen and searched up mist and smoke.

Something splashed on the virtual screen, but he ignored it. He moved closer, and her body tingled. Sexual energy thrived in this area, or did it thrive because of their presence?

She didn't know why, but she wanted to touch him. Maybe

it was the fantastical ambience of the creek, the way the gentle water moved and dripped, forming a melody that hypnotized her. The subtle teal mist that lingered with the white smoke created the perfect backdrop for the stirrings in her heart.

As her fingers moved from his face, down his neck, his dark green skin tone fluctuated. Did she do that to him?

"Your skin changes color." This wasn't the first she'd seen him react to her.

"Only when I'm extremely aroused." Gray eyes grew molten, and she wanted his mouth on her.

She pressed her lips to his. His mouth firm and smooth over hers, tantalizing her. Their tongues met, exploring each other. His hand cupped the back of her neck, angling her mouth so he could dive deeper. He kissed like a god who knew how to conquer.

Heat liquefied in her core, shot up her thighs and spiraled to every corner of her body. She moaned a protest when his mouth left hers, skimming along her jaw and down her neck. Her veins pulsed, and his lips suckled like they craved the throbbing.

The scent of wood, earth, and musky desire teased her nose. She inhaled Jarzell's scent that made her feel safe and bold.

Desire warred in her. He lit that fire in her, encouraging her to take what she wanted with no fear of repercussion. She had never felt this powerful force in her before. She needed to be careful. A power like this could destroy her.

Rita pulled back. "You're an excellent kisser."

"So are you." His eyes intensified, and the pupils shifted again.

"Something is pushing us together," she said.

"Seems wise to listen to it." He licked his lips with a green tongue that was tipped with orange.

Rita's finger touched the corner of his mouth and slid across his bottom lip. "Your tongue changes color too?"

"You did that." His tongue emerged from his mouth and met her index finger. The slickness and softness of the green tip turned orange.

Heat shot through her. She loved the fact that she could affect him like that.

"I have other areas that change colors too." He smiled.

The vivid image popped into her mind and fired up her skin. This time, she didn't cover her face.

"We can explore that another time." He twirled a purple lock of her hair around his finger. "I want to know if your body changes color the way your lovely face does."

Rita laughed. "It doesn't change color." Well, not that she knew of. If she did, her exes had never mentioned it.

Was their relationship moving too fast? Though she'd accepted her attraction to Jarzell, she had to take careful steps. Her relationship to Philip had started out as a quick and powerful attraction that moved too swiftly for her to see any defects. When there was too much passion, it blinded everything else.

She turned to the screen, and the data intrigued her. "Can this be true about mist and smoke? They're considered intelligent entities? One came from fire, the other from water, or rather moisture."

Jarzell opened another screen. "They represent two important elements of nature. Saedo values nature very much. You can see it in how we treat our land. We give it love and respect, and it flourishes for us."

That was one of the reasons why she loved living here. If only humans did the same to Earth, who knew what magic and medicine could emerge from that love and appreciation?

She swiped to a new page with information. "This site says the mist and smoke can travel between the seen and unseen worlds. Like powerful messengers." Rita's finger stopped at one sentence that chilled her bones.

Heat is a messenger from the Smoke Realm.

Was that the reason for the unfamiliar heat in her body? It could explain why the body-reader didn't register the increased body temperature. This heat came from a different dimension.

What message did the smoke have for Rita?

There was no dismissing the fact that Rita and Jarzell had an inexplicable bond. That was part of what thrilled and frightened her the most. He hadn't mentioned anything about her being his starmate. But she read the acknowledgment in his eyes. Maybe he needed time to let that sink in. She needed time to absorb all of this as well.

Was her connection to Jarzell something more than just being starmates?

She looked over at him. "I'm ready to go to Grandma Ova now."

ELEVEN

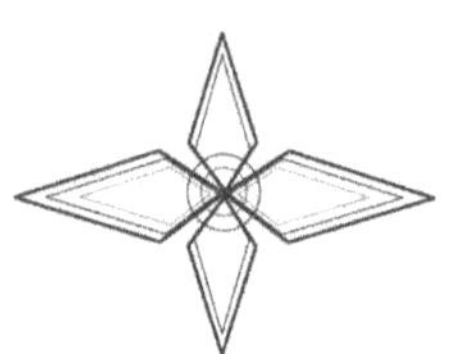

Rita called Grandma Ova to let her know they were on their way over, but she didn't pick up. She was probably busy working in her many gardens.

"We should have called her earlier. I don't like arriving unannounced at someone's home."

"She won't mind. Everyone in Saedo knows and loves Grandma Ova. She's like everyone's grandmother. Citizens from all over the villages travel to her home to retrieve fruits, vegetables, and herbs. She took a break when she injured her legs, but she's recovered now." Jarzell pressed a button on his sports rider and pulled up a virtual screen, checking on some data.

The Province of Saedo consisted of several villages. Rita and her siblings lived in the Main Village, which was more like a large suburb, and the Village Center was like the downtown area crammed with business.

"I'll leave her a message, anyway. It's the courteous thing to do," Rita said.

"This is odd." Jarzell swiped to a different screen displaying a diagram she didn't understand.

She was about to ask him what the image was when white smoke streamed across the windshield of his sports rider, stopping in front of Rita, long enough for her to notice it. But it was the strong cedrus scent that alerted her attention. She'd gotten used to the smoky and woodsy aroma that calmed her.

"Do you see the white smoke?" Rita kept her gaze on the smoke that moved and lingered at the edge of the forest.

Jarzell flicked his gaze up and sniffed. He clicked off the virtual screen, gripped the steering wheel, and pulled over to the side of the road. A few personal riders, sports riders, and longships hovered by, but this particular road wasn't as busy as the others.

They both got out of the rider. "Look." She pointed to the smoke that trailed into the forest.

Heat bloomed from her chest, spreading like roots to other areas of her. If heat was the messenger from the Smoke Realm, then what did this smoke want her to know?

Rita prepared to follow it. "The smoke is probably a clue to the missing tablet."

The heat, smoke, and cedrus scent were puzzle pieces that slowly came together for her.

Agreeing, Jarzell and Rita entered the forest. She'd lived here for months, and this was her first time in Saedo's forest. As a child, she loved hiking and enjoyed the silence of nature. She glanced at the variety of trees greeting her. She found trees that resembled pine, cypress, oak, maple, and others on Earth. However, the shapes and colors of the leaves were different.

The energy of the forest differed from that of Derwood Creek. An uncomfortable feeling slid across her skin, making her shiver. Was it a good idea to follow the smoke?

"There's a strong cedar scent that way." Jarzell made a right turn and began walking.

She stepped on dirt, pebbles, and grass, trying to catch up to him. His long legs ate the distance fast. "Wait up."

He stopped, and an apologetic look graced his face. "Sorry, I'm so used to moving fast."

"I can see that. You're very focused."

"Concentration helps keep distractions at bay. That's how I've been able to accomplish projects and close cases. If there's something I need to do, I don't hesitate."

Nothing appeared out of the ordinary, but the cedrus scent remained.

"Were you always like this?" She tried to imagine growing up with someone whose body and brain moved with swiftness.

Jarzell looked at her. "Yes. There was a point when I could've been inspired to adjust."

"What happened?"

He hesitated a brief moment, and that stung her. She had shared a private part of her life with him, and she hoped he would do the same. They were on a different playing field now, weren't they? Maybe her speculation was wrong.

"If you're uncomfortable, it's fine. I was just—"

"I'm not uncomfortable, Rita. It's been a while since I've discussed my personal life with anyone. You entered my life and switched gears for me." The honesty on his face removed the sting. "I was used to doing things one way, but wondered if I should adapt to a new way."

Rita smiled. "Change is a good thing, no?" She knew all about adjusting to change. She lived on an undiscovered planet and had developed powerful feelings for an alien. That was a massive change. That was the kind of story that existed in science fiction or fantasy books. But as an artist who saw things with various perspectives, she welcomed the unconventional route.

"At this moment, change is very good. But back then, I wasn't sure."

Now she really wanted to know what had occurred in his previous relationship.

He reached out a hand, tucking an errant strand of hair behind her ear. He opened his mouth to say something, but a growl erupted near them. He shifted his body, a simple move full of menace, urging her behind him as he surveyed the area. The tactful skills ingrained in a soldier came alive as he gripped his blaster, scanning the area.

A cold knot tightened in her stomach as more growls sounded. Rita and Jarzell strode in that direction. Though fear bubbled in Rita, she felt safe beside Jarzell.

The stream of white smoke appeared up ahead beside a ribbon of teal mist. "Look at them. It's like they're guiding us."

The way the mist and smoke behaved made Rita believe they possessed a personality.

"I've never seen anything like that before. Let's follow them."

The growls became louder and echoed through the forest. Jarzell lifted his hand, signaling for her to stop moving. The white smoke and teal mist disappeared.

Jarzell and Rita moved toward the sounds, watching their steps and trying not to make any noises. They came to flat ground but couldn't see any wild animals. What made all those eerie sounds?

The dirt shifted beneath Rita's feet, and Jarzell drew her away from the threat. She looked at him, appreciating the way he took care of her without hesitation.

"Stay here," he said. His expression zeroed in on the puddle forming where she had stood.

The puddle increased to about three feet in diameter, making it more like a well of black water. A whirlpool spun at the center, creating a portal. As the water spun, it sucked in the life force of the surrounding vegetation. The grass and flowers dried up, and the pebbles and rocks lost their luster. They looked lifeless, which was an odd way of describing inanimate objects, but she didn't know how else to describe the cracked and crumbly rocks that had no character left.

Growls echoed from the spinning well, and a creature flew out of it, landing close to Rita's feet. She backed away and tripped over a branch on the ground, falling onto her butt. The creature looked like a crossbreed between a wolf and bear. It glared at her with its bulging red eyes as its long, spiky tail curled.

Jarzell rushed toward Rita, but the massive beast jumped in and blocked him from her.

"Flekken!" A vehement curse exploded out of him. He aimed at the creature, blasting at it. It jumped, and he missed.

The creature snarled at Jarzell and then Rita. "I'm going to rip you apart and feed you to my children." The mother beast howled, and three smaller versions of her emerged from the woods. Another two crawled out from the dark well.

These were the same Ulkrin beasts that attacked Sasha and Inga. She'd seen images of them splashed all over the village news. The horrid beasts gave off a nauseating smell that churned her stomach.

The offspring responded with delighted growls. Fear crippled Rita as she scooted away, scraping her palms on the rocks. Her back hit a tree trunk as she dug for courage, and pushed herself up, standing flush against the tree. Heat radiated from her body, and she began to sweat. She couldn't tell if it was anxiety producing the heat or if it was the odd body temperature fluctuations she'd been experiencing lately.

It didn't matter. She had to find something to defend herself. Heat wasn't going to help. She glanced over at Jarzell, who was blasting away at the mother beast with no success. The creature moved with such a swift speed, it appeared abnormal. A smaller creature flung itself at Jarzell and bit him on the shoulder. *Shit.*

"Jarzell!" Rita shouted as terror gripped her.

Jarzell fired at its head and rushed over to her, but the mother beast prevented him from reaching Rita's side, whipping her spiky tail at him.

A tree branch from the ground caught Rita's attention, and she reached down, gripping it like a bat.

One of the offspring charged at Rita, and she whacked it, sending it to the ground. The sound that erupted confirmed something had cracked within the creature. A smile tugged at Rita's lips. Two more offspring appeared before her. White smoke slithered in front of Rita as teal mist surrounded Jarzell. The scent of cedrus filled her nose as heat increased in her body. She prayed for a sudden rainstorm to cool her from the heat.

Why was she so damn hot right now?

Oh, God, please keep Jarzell safe. I don't want to lose him. He's made me feel alive again; made me believe that I'm worth something.

Why was she thinking such morbid thoughts?

Twenty feet away, Jarzell whipped a curious glance at her before blasting the mother beast. "My brothers are on their way."

Heat traveled to her arms, hands, and fingers. Her body shuddered from the onslaught. Despite that, she held the bat in her hand like a baseball player ready to defend; ready to win. A strange courage surged in her. This opportunity to fight for her life had changed the way her mind worked. Unlike the car accident that had tossed her into a firestorm where she had no control, this unstable moment gave her a chance to take control.

That little difference affected Rita. She didn't feel useless or that she couldn't take care of herself.

Jarzell rushed over and place a hand on her arm, concern flashing in his eyes. "You okay?"

She nodded. The mother beast jumped in front of them, blood dripping from her face, neck, and legs. Why wasn't she dead? The pungent odor of blood and beast stung her eyes. She pushed back the nausea that wanted to come out.

The beast growled at her. "We've got plans for all of you, especially the humans. You stole them from us."

The way Jarzell stepped in front of her—the way in which he protected her—moved her more than she realized. It was as if a sudden earthquake erupted from within her heart, shifting the tectonic plates of her soul.

No man had ever cared for her this way, and Jarzell had shown it more than once.

Rita clutched the tree branch tighter, skin pressing into the hard surface of the bark. She was ready to fight beside her man. Yes, Jarzell was hers. She claimed him as her own. A power she didn't understand escalated in her. Heat surged through her fingers and onto the tree branch. Smoke seeped from the bark and filled the area. The cedrus scent spiked, and her body shuddered from the powerful aroma.

All at once, the mother beast and her offspring prepared to charge at them. Rita tightened her grip on her bat-branch, while Jarzell blasted. The offspring sniffed the air as white smoke attacked their noses. A second later, the offspring dropped to the ground, unable to move.

The mother beast snarled and swung her claw at the smoke. The smoke dispersed the way vapors do. But the smoke increased in density every time she swiped at it. When her claw covered her nose, Rita understood and whipped her attention to Jarzell.

"They don't like cedrus scent."

The mother beast howled, but the cry was weaker than before. Jarzell sent a slew of blasts into her. Her body thudded to the ground and pungent odor increased like it was a pheromone informing the others about her death.

More growls emerged from the dark well that spun, collecting the surrounding vegetation.

"We need to close that damn portal." Jarzell shot into it, and the blast returned, almost hitting him.

Her heart knocked against her chest at the close call.

"Someone's manipulating dark energy," he said.

White smoke flowed around the portal. "I have an idea." Rita wasn't sure if it would work, but she had to try. She gripped the tree branch. With her mind, she visualized the increased smoke and cedrus scent. The vision became real as smoke covered the branch. The potent scent of cedrus became too much for her nose and eyes. Satisfied, she whipped the branch into the whirlpool. It swallowed the branch into the abyss.

Awful noises erupted, and Jarzell pulled Rita against him, moving away from the danger. He turned, so that his back faced the whirlpool. He became the shield, protecting her from whatever could fly out of that dark pit.

Emotions surged in her, and she placed a gentle hand over his chest. He glanced over his shoulder. "Stay here. I need to kill them."

He didn't give her a chance to reply. Her focused star-being —a man with a mission—stepped over to the dark well and positioned himself in a defensive stance. Five creatures climbed out from the hole with sharp claws and long tongues. The heinous beasts were a different breed from the other Ulkrin creatures. These possessed spikes along the back and two mouths with sharp fangs. They weren't as big as the mother beast though.

Jarzell blasted them, but the energy blasts didn't affect

them. These beasts appeared stronger than the other creatures. Rita waved her hand, intentionally collecting the smoke and cedrus scent. They accumulated around her as she'd hoped. Then she pushed them toward the beasts, praying they'd kill the beasts before Jarzell got hurt.

Unlike the other Ulkrin creatures, these beasts were impervious to the smoke and cedrus. Confidence crumbled as disappointment clutched her stomach. One creature jumped onto her back and raked its claws into her skin.

Into her scar.

Pain shot through her, but the heat overwhelmed her more. The clash of heat and something else warred inside her. Her body wanted to burst. Her vision blurred, and all sounds collided into one. She couldn't collapse, and fought to stand strong. Jarzell needed her help.

The blood-soaked shirt clung to her back as her equilibrium wavered, and her body dropped to the ground. The metallic scent of fresh blood smothered her senses.

More blasts sounded. Voices erupted, or was that her ears hearing things?

"Rita! Are you all right? My brothers are here. Stay with me."

Was that Jarzell?

She couldn't move, and her vision grew foggy. Arms wrapped around her, but she couldn't see who it was. Needles stabbed her back. Was the creature still biting her? A sharp pain coursed through her, and she blacked out.

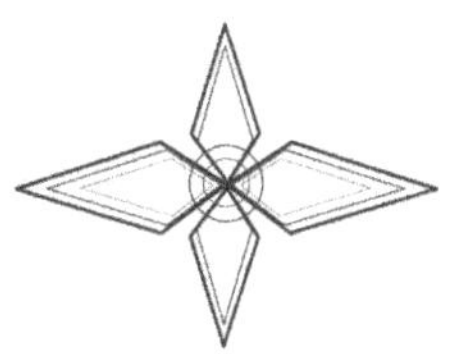

Voices drummed around Rita, but she couldn't open her eyes to see who was there. She recognized Jarzell's voice speaking to Grandma Ova and one of his brothers. The conversation sounded distant, but she sensed their energies nearby.

The scent of cedar swirled around her nose. "Follow me. Follow the smoke." The gentle voice whispered in her ears.

Glowing smoke floated across the darkness of her vision like a bright nebula moving across space. She reached out a hand and touched the smoke. Upon contact, she was transported across space, flying with the smoke as it kept her afloat. Was she dreaming? She felt like she was in between states of consciousness.

She blinked and stood in a dark forest with only a few trees illuminated. Everything else became a blur. She smelled the wet dirt and the cedrus trees. The significance of cedrus was something she had to investigate. Of all trees, why did she connect to the cedrus?

Darkness surrounded her, but she wasn't afraid. This was the dark that reminded her of a lovely summer night. And though she should be scared, a sense of warmth and safety embraced her, as if unseen arms guided her way.

Where was Jarzell? Was he safe?

As she stepped barefoot on the soil, wetness seeped into the soles of her feet. In front of her, images of her past formed within the smoke patterns in the air. The car accident, the fire, the scent of burning flesh, the sensation of fire chewing her skin, and the panic that had crippled her in that moment flashed past like images from a movie.

Emotions rose as tears flowed from her eyes. She saw her parents, and the longing for them choked her. More tears came. An image of Philip leaving her apartment also came to the forefront. Then the movie froze like fossilization or calcification. Tears spilled over, dripping on her hand. She stared at the blue teardrops as the teal mist rose up from them and floated next to the white smoke.

Jarzell. He was the mist, and she was the smoke. The bizarre occurrence stunned her.

She had to be dreaming. She pinched herself, and discomfort radiated from the spot on her arm. Could she be experiencing a lucid dream? She'd read up on lucid dreams where people knew they were dreaming and could make decisions, therefore steering the dream to a different outcome. Was this it?

If not, she couldn't explain it at all. Her back ached, and she remembered an Ulkrin creature had clawed her skin. Was she hallucinating?

The cedar scent intensified, wanting her attention. She focused on the smoke and the single ribbon of teal mist accompanying her. The smoke led to a giant cedrus tree. Right next to it was a cedar tree from Earth. As she approached, she noticed a crack in the trunk. She placed a palm over it, remembering how it had saved her during the accident. If the cedar tree hadn't stopped her car from rolling down the huge ditch, she would have been killed instantly.

Thank you.

Warmth brushed her cheek in confirmation of her gratitude.

The scent became prominent when more smoke seeped from the bark of both the cedar and cedrus trees. As she stared at them, an epiphany illuminated in her mind.

These trees were the same family: one existed on Earth, and the other lived in Saedo. The cedar possessed green leaves, while the cedrus possessed blue leaves.

"Thank you for being here, Rita. We've been waiting for you."

Waiting for her? How did it know her name? Where did the voice come from?

She couldn't tell if the voice was male or female. But wisdom stirred in the calm tones. She didn't know how she understood that. She just did.

"I don't understand. Why were you waiting for me? Who are you?"

"We're ancestors of this land. Our 'family' has kept you safe because it knew we needed you here." The green leaves from the cedar tree rustled.

Rita stared at it. She was having a conversation with Saedo ancestors via trees. She should be surprised, but after everything she'd witnessed, it fascinated her even more. She'd always gravitated toward strange and inexplicable things, and now they were all around her.

"When you and your sisters entered Saedo, you brought fresh energies that activated the dormant energies within the land. We knew you'd be important in protecting Saedo. This land is sacred, and it's now being threatened."

"By the Ulkrins?"

"Yes, and those who want the wisdom seeped within this land."

Did the voice actually come from the tree? At first, she thought it did, but the way it echoed made it appear as though it was everywhere and nowhere at the same time. It was a silly question, but she had to ask it.

"Are you speaking to me from inside the trees?"

"We are energies, so we are here, there, everywhere."

Star-being spirits.

Rita remembered how the villagers had welcomed her and her sisters. "Thank you for welcoming us onto your land."

"That's how it should be everywhere. It is love that thrives in Saedo. You and your sisters activated a new love between star-beings and humans."

Rita's mind sparked. "So star-beings haven't fallen in love with humans before us."

"They have. But the love you and your starmate—your forever mate—share differs from those that came before. Your energies react to each other like rare chemistry, and that reaction births a new frequency, a new version of the love that vibrates at a higher level. Your love empowers the energy of Saedo, and that's attracting enemies."

She tried to grasp the idea of how something as beautiful and precious as love could pose a danger to anyone. How could love attract enemies? Logically, it didn't make sense because more love meant more light, right? So how could anything bad happen around an abundance of love?

But on a skewed level—one she didn't know how she understood—she recognized that massive treasures attracted greed, just like gems attracted pirates.

Terror squirmed in her stomach as she pondered what the Ulkrins would do to gain this treasured land. "How are we supposed to fight them?"

"You'll know what to do."

The streams of smoke formed into a face of an old female star-being with long flowing sparkly hair. But that face soon morphed into a male star-being. The faces kept changing, and for a moment, they even appeared like animals on the land.

"Can you be more specific?" Rita asked.

The smoke laughed, and that was when she realized there was more than one voice. But when they spoke in unison, it emerged as one sound. The laughter was what clued her in.

"Work together to fight it. We'll be at your side to assist you. The family has awakened."

"Family? What do you mean?"

"Find the Sacred Tablet. The answers are there."

"Do you know where it is? Can you tell me?"

"That's not how things work. We can't tell you because that would affect the law of free will. Nature speaks in metaphors. We must follow those laws too. The tablet is waiting for *you*."

"Why me?"

"Because your energy activated it. How many times have you stared at it, trying to decipher its wisdom? It saw you, it heard you. It knows your story. Find it."

They made it sound so easy. "I have no clue where to start."

"You already have what you need. Go find it with Jarzell. This journey is for both of you. That's why the tablet is missing."

What did that mean?

At that moment, the ribbon of teal mist surged in density around her.

"What you thought were scars are the marks of strength. Remember that."

A massive cloud of white smoke and teal mist spun around her, yanking her somewhere she couldn't see. The swift spinning made her dizzy, so she closed her eyes.

When she opened them, she was sitting up in bed with Jarzell and Grandma Ova staring at her.

"Hi. Welcome back." Jarzell's smile was all she needed to ground her.

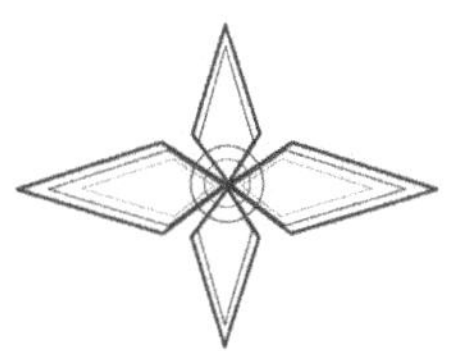

THIRTEEN

Rita scooted over to make room for Jarzell on the bed, which appeared to be inside Grandma Ova's home.

"Are you feeling all right?" He searched her face, arms, and legs with his worried gaze.

The concerned look reflected on Grandma Ova's face. Had Jarzell brought her to Grandma Ova's after the battle? Had she fainted from loss of blood?

"Did I pass out?"

"You did," Jarzell said. "My brothers arrived just in time to help fight those hybrid monsters. Grandma Ova was on her way back from the Village Center and also stopped. She patched up your wounds, and we brought you back to her place for closer examination."

Grandma Ova placed down a tray by the side table with an herbal drink and a bowl of soup. "You've been unconscious for five hours. Well, you woke, but you weren't really here."

Confused, Rita looked at Jarzell and back at Grandma Ova.

Grandma Ova offered a warm smile. "You woke—or rather —you were in a different realm for a couple of hours. Eat the soup and drink the herbal tea, it'll help rebalance your body. We'll talk about your astral-travel in the morning."

Rita traveled to another dimension? How was that even possible? It explained why everything had seemed so real and so... different. She had so many questions, but exhaustion weighed on her. She flicked a glance out through the window across from her. It was dark outside.

"You're healing quickly with none of my remedies. But you'll heal even faster with them. I'll check your wound again tomorrow."

Rita glanced down at the cotton shirt and pants Grandma Ova had changed her into. This meant Grandma Ova had seen Rita's scars. Had Jarzell seen them too? Embarrassment whirled in her. No one had seen her scars besides her doctors, siblings, and Philip. She'd thought she had time to prepare herself for that kind of revelation. She imagined the scars were even worse after that creature clawed at her. Fatigue was probably the reason for her self-consciousness.

One look at Rita and Grandma Ova understood. "I've seen all kinds of wounds in all kinds of places. There's no need for any embarrassment." She glanced at Jarzell. "Am I right?"

He hesitated, raking a hand through his hair. "Y-yes. There's no need to be embarrassed." He got up from the bed and poured himself a glass of blue water.

Why did *he* look embarrassed?

"We had to remove the poison from your back before it seeped into your bloodstream. I don't think you realize how beautiful your scars are. Jarzell can show you an image of them later."

Beautiful? Were they crazy?

They didn't need to show her; she knew what her scars looked like. Knowing that Jarzell had seen her back made her cheeks flame with embarrassment. She'd been imagining him doing all kinds of intimate things to her, so why was she so embarrassed about this?

Relationships confused her. It made her feel indecisive, not knowing what she wanted. Did she want him to touch and see every part of her *except* her back? How silly was that?

You can only kiss me from the front. Stay away from my back view.

Rita laughed as she envisioned her demand with Jarzell while they were being intimate. *Ridiculous.*

After the way he protected her in the forest, she should know better. He'd probably seen worse wounds from the battles he'd been in. She forced herself to stop caring about what anyone thought of her. She didn't want to be stuck in the past.

Despite that, there was a special bond between them, and his opinion mattered to her. Revelation hit her. She was falling for him, whether she wanted to or not. A part of her fought it off, but another part pushed her forward.

The truth always found its way to the front. Now, it looked her square in the eye.

As if he sensed she was thinking about him, his gaze met hers. Questions swam in his eyes as he stared at her, sending her heart rate skyrocketing.

They had an unfinished conversation to complete. He was going to tell her about his past relationship when that dark well had emerged, spitting out those horrid creatures. She also wanted to know why he blushed just now. Not to mention his interest in her sketches of him. But, all of those things could wait. There were more critical matters at hand.

"We need to find the Sacred Tablet. It's going to help us fight the Ulkrins. Your ancestors told me that," Rita tried shifting the pillows behind her back, but had trouble. Jarzell came over to help and sat back down beside her. The familiar musky scent of him made her feel safe.

"I could tell," Grandma Ova smiled. "The ancestors don't reveal themselves to just anyone. Consider yourself fortunate. I don't sense the tablet is in danger." She rose up from her chair and placed a hand on Rita's forehead, a parental and caring gesture that Rita had missed.

"The ancestors told me to work with Jarzell to find the Sacred Tablet."

"We'll search for it." Jarzell placed a hand over hers, and energy rushed down her spine, creating all kinds of wild images in her mind.

How could he excite her like this when she was in bed recovering from a horrible attack?

"The Sacred Tablet is important, but so is your health. If you're not well, how will you find it?" Grandma Ova gave her a look a mother gives to her children when reminding them of what was important. "Jarzell told me about a dark well that emerged from the ground. The Ulkrins are working with someone who knows how to manipulate dark energy and who has knowledge of the different dimensions. This is probably the same person who sent those energetic clouds that created the alien storm."

Concern stabbed at Rita for the star-beings who welcomed her and her sisters. "The Ulkrins won't stop until we kill them." That fact would require more battles.

Rita recalled how she had whacked the Ulkrin beasts with the bat-branch without even thinking. She wasn't a killer, but fear for her life, and Jarzell's, pushed her to defend them. She acknowledged the symbolism in her action. She took control of her life in that critical moment. The concept wasn't complicated, nor should it be. But it had taken her a while to find the courage to do it.

She had been lost in her own darkness and depression for so long she had forgotten how freeing it was to take back the power she had over her own life, scars and all. She could do that on a new planet. She stole a glance at Jarzell while he studied something on his wristband. When she fought beside him, this innate courage and renewed confidence in herself surfaced in a way she hadn't sensed before.

Could Jarzell be the reason for her healing?

"Chief Mozar is setting up emergency centers for all villages." Jarzell typed something on the small screen. "My brothers will assist with those. We need to inform and train the citizens who can fight back in case something happens."

Grandma Ova nodded. "That's a wonderful plan. Being prepared will boost everyone's confidence." She turned to Rita. "You can sleep in this guest room tonight. The bathroom is over there. You can access my garden through that door if you want some fresh air." She pointed to the door near the back wall. "In fact, I highly recommend it. The sweet aroma from the pink grass would help your body heal too. Rest up, and I'll see you tomorrow."

Rita shifted and didn't feel the discomfort she expected from the attack she received. "Did you put something on my back? I don't feel any pain or anything."

The wise woman smiled. "There's a healing balm on your back. The herbal tea and soup will aid your body's recovery. You'll be fine."

After Grandma Ova left, Jarzell grabbed the cup of herbal tea. "Drink this." She assumed he was going to give her the cup, but he held it in his hands. "Open up. I want to make sure you drink it *now*, rather than later."

She arched an eyebrow at the commanding tone, and he sighed. "You need to heal."

The attentive gesture startled her more. Rita opened her mouth and drank the sweet tea. She kept her gaze on him over the rim of the cup. After he made sure she had ingested enough of the medicinal tea, he placed it back on the side table.

"Did I do a good job, *doctor?*" She'd never been tended like this before. She *loved* it.

He smiled. "That's a new term for me. Just trying to take care of you."

"Do you think I don't take care of myself?" she retorted.

"I'm sure you do. But I don't think you've been pampered enough. There's nothing wrong with me pampering you."

Was he saying that because he saw her scars? Did he pity her?

Her face probably showed all those emotions because he tipped up her chin, so their eyes aligned. "I'm not the pampering type, but *you* make me want to take care of you, put you first. I don't like seeing you in danger or hurt like this."

Put you first. The door to her heart blasted open from the unexpected emotion.

No man had ever said those words to her. But this stunning star-being had not only said them, he proved them in action. She remembered how he had shoved himself in front of her, shielding her from danger. "Thanks for keeping me safe back there. I appreciate it."

He traced a finger along her lips. "You were concerned about me too. I heard you praying for me."

She did? Rita flipped back through her mind, replaying the events in her head.

Oh, God, please keep Jarzell safe. I don't want to lose him. He's made me feel alive again; made me believe that I'm worth something.

Rita recalled the terror that overwhelmed her in that moment. She hadn't wanted to lose the person who gave her hope.

"The creatures were all around you," she said softly. "I was terrified for you."

"Is that all?" His stare intensified with a seriousness she didn't understand. What did he want her to say?

His face was so close to hers, and his musky scent teased her senses. She shouldn't be this aroused, considering her body was just attacked hours ago. All she had to do was move a centimeter, and his lips would be on hers.

"Besides my mother—who is no longer alive—no female has ever prayed for me." His face softened as he gripped her hand, placing it over his chest. "It warms my corra that you care so much for me."

"You care for me too."

"Protecting is what I'm trained to do as a Saedo soldier. But when this threat came so close to you, this powerful urge to shelter you mounted in me. It came from a deep place I didn't understand. Your safety was more important than mine." The rawness of his words reflected on his face.

She squeezed his hand.

He squeezed back. "When you collapsed in my arms, terror gripped me. I've never been that scared in my life. I thought I was losing you. I'll never forget that horrible feeling. It was only when Grandma Ova assured me that you'd be fine that I relaxed."

These strong emotions for each other confused her. They hadn't known each other long enough for such deep-seated feelings. Rita had to be cautious because she didn't want her heart shattered again. But what about him? Was he cautious too? Or was he overanalyzing everything?

There was one thing she knew for certain. She wanted to kiss him. She inched closer and pressed her lips to his. "I think we should take it easy." She pressed more kisses to his face. "Don't analyze anything." She moved to his jaw and the color of his green skin fluctuated. "Just go with our feelings and see where that takes us."

"I agree." He gripped her face with both hands, kissing her the way the suns kisses the planets, the way the wind kisses the leaves.

When he broke the kiss, she was both invigorated and breathless. She just got a dose of some life-inducing aphrodisiac that benefited her, but also took something from her.

The smile on his face showed he received what he wanted.

"You should eat the soup and get some rest. I'm going to change out of these clothes."

The thought of him leaving to go home pricked at her. "I'll see you tomorrow, then?"

"I'm not going home. I'm staying in the other guest room. I'm not leaving until your back is healed."

"Don't you have to work tomorrow?"

"My work schedule is flexible. Right now, my job is to find the Sacred Tablet, and how I divide up my time is up to me. Have the soup."

"You're so bossy."

He flashed a charming smile. "Not bossy, just making sure you eat."

Rita gripped the spoon and scooped some of the warm soup into her mouth. "Happy?"

"Yes, very. I'll be back."

She preferred this sudden burst of energy over the exhaustion from when she first woke up. Now her mind could explore what she experienced in the dream state or "astral-travel" as Grandma Ova stated. What did the creature do to her scars?

FOURTEEN

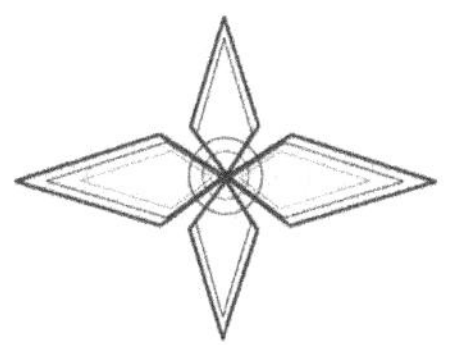

WHEN JARZELL RETURNED, he wore a set of comfy, white pajamas that looked like the set Grandma Ova had left on the top of the drawer for her. His wet hair showed he'd just taken a quick shower. She didn't know why, but the casualness of his washed hair and the contrast of his damp green skin against the white sleepwear gave her a new definition of sexy.

He glanced at the empty bowl of soup. "Do you want more or something else to eat?"

She got off the bed, expecting an imbalance, so she lingered.

He looked her up and down while she stood beside the bed. "Is your equilibrium okay?"

To her surprise, her balance was stable, and her mobility quicker than normal. Not only that, her flexibility was greatly improved. She stretched her arms up and bent over to touch her toes. She wasn't completely out of shape, but she had never been able to touch her toes unless she'd practiced yoga for months, and she hadn't done that in at least a year.

Whatever remedy Grandma Ova had given her, Rita wanted more of it.

She clutched the tray and prepared to bring it out to the

kitchen. "No, thanks. I need a shower to wash off all the filth from today. When I come back, I'd like to see the video of my scars."

"You go shower, I'll take care of this." He grabbed the tray from her hands.

Fifteen minutes later, Rita returned to her room, and the sweet breeze drifting from the open window relaxed her body immediately. Jarzell must've opened the window beside the bed, letting in the fragrance. Was this the scent of the pink grass Grandma Ova mentioned? Light glowed from the door that led out to the back garden.

Rita found Jarzell standing at the wooden railing, staring out at the garden filled with shrubberies with glowing berries. She strode up to him and inhaled the fresh air.

"That's some healing grass." Rita looked over at the field of pink grass glittering in the distance. Their tips sparkled like a sea of stars below the night sky. The spectacular view along with the aroma calmed her mind and body.

He turned to her. "Did the shower help? How are you feeling now?"

"Refreshed. Thanks."

Flowers from the nearby bushes and dangling vines lit up the deck, casting a soft glow on Jarzell's face. Her heart thudded, and her thighs tightened as she studied his features. The soft light illuminated part of his face, leaving the rest of it in shadows that added more depth and mystery to his character. The dark features tugged at her, like an invitation to something dangerous and decadent. This was the kind of proposal she used to yearn for; the kind that offered a delicious, unexpected adventure. It was like she stepped into one of her creative modes that allowed limitless freedom to explore and, at the same time, to know that she was completely safe.

"It's beautiful out here." The constellation in the sky caught her attention. Were these the same star clusters that were visible from Earth?

"You've made it more captivating. You're beautiful, you know that?" Jarzell twirled a lock of her purple hair around his finger.

This was the second time that adjective was used to describe her. It had been a long time since she believed in such a word. "It's hard not to believe it when you say it."

"I don't lie."

Warmth kindled in her heart. People had said she was beautiful. But did she feel it? Not really. Not after the scars. It didn't matter what she appeared like on the surface or how she dressed up with makeup and clothes, she felt ugly and unworthy after the fire desecrated her skin. It had destroyed her self-esteem. She knew there were people worse off than herself in the world, where they had far more visible scars. But depression had a power that crippled the mind in inexplicable ways.

His honesty shifted something in her. "I appreciate that more than you know."

"When we rescued you and your sisters, some of my brothers commented on you."

They did? What about Jarzell? Did he say anything about her?

Jarzell answered her as if he saw into her mind. "I agreed with them. But you seemed like you wanted to be left alone. Then I had to travel for work. My mist kept showing me images of your face, like it wanted me to meet you. So when the Sacred Tablet went missing, I knew that was a sign for me."

"Are you saying the tablet went missing because it wanted us to meet?"

"Why not? I've learned to expect the unexpected."

"That sounds romantic, but I think it's hiding because of something that could hurt all of Saedo. We're not that special."

"Speak for yourself. I'm *outstanding*. You like what you see, you know it. Admit it."

She laughed as the tangled emotions she had felt in the beginning untangled themselves. Tonight, the ambience and sweet aroma seduced her to do something spontaneous.

"I do."

His eyes sparked with a dare. "What are you going to do about it, Creatress?"

"Something 'outstanding.'" She tossed back a challenge of her own. "But first, I need to see the video."

On cue, he flipped on a virtual screen from his wristband. "Let's sit down for this."

Rita sat down in a chair with a soft cushion, and Jarzell took the seat beside her.

In the video, Rita lay unconscious on the bed with her bare back full of scars and blood. A ghost of an injury revealed where the creature had attacked her. She had expected a large gash from the pain that had shot through her during the attack, but from the look of things, the wound didn't appear all that bad.

The smoke seeping through her scars shocked her more. Grandma Ova waved a large leaf that was twice the size of her palm over Rita's back. The large leaf absorbed the smoke, turning its green color into gray. The gray portions broke apart like soot and fell into a bowl.

Rita shot him a puzzled look. "What happened to the leaf?"

"The smoke pushed the poison out of your body, and the leaf sucked it up. Grandma Ova feared the poisonous smoke could cause unforeseen damages to the area. The Ulkrin hybrids have a lethal venom on their claws. You were fortunate that it didn't damage your body. What I didn't understand was that your skin was cool to the touch, yet smoke emerged from your body like it was on fire."

The scars that used to spread across her back had shrunk in size.

"What did Grandma Ova put on my back? I've never seen skin heal that quickly."

"She sprayed a healing balm on your back, but she claims that's not why you healed so fast. The smoke escalated your healing by stopping the poison from entering your bloodstream. It burned the poison inside you."

The video ended, and Jarzell turned off the screen.

"I've been experiencing a strange heat for at least a week. It became more prominent the day you came by the Village Library."

"Grandma Ova said the smoke isn't from here. Not from this dimension. She'll tell us about it tomorrow."

Where did the smoke come from? A ribbon of teal mist emerged from the pores on his neck, shoulders, and arms. It flowed over to her arm. She waved her fingers through it. Did the smoke and the mist come from the same place?

After witnessing the smoke seeping through her scars, she saw her car accident in a different way. "This might sound strange, but I think the smoke from the fire saved me. Maybe it protected me from worse injuries, and the energy in Saedo lured it out?"

"I don't think that sounds strange at all. It makes sense. Maybe it's a sacred lore that connects Earth to Celeron. We don't know the vastness of the Cosmos or what it has planned for us. We can sit here all day and dissect it, but the true reason as to why and how things happen are meant to be discovered in their own time. Just like me and you." He skimmed his thumb along her bottom lip.

Her insides turned hot and liquid. "I never expected to meet someone on this planet, but now that I've met you, I can't stop myself from wanting you. It's been a long time."

The corner of his lips quirked. "Tell me what you want, Creatress, and I'll make it happen."

"That'll make you the Creator."

"The Creator and Creatress," he repeated. "I like the sound of that. I'm not an artist though, but I *am* very good with my hands." He waved his long and powerful fingers, and heat burst from her core.

An onslaught of images flashed across her mind, wiping away all proper thoughts except for the ones with his naked body on hers. She forgot their entire conversation before this moment. She forgot how to breathe. She forgot how a decent woman should act. At this moment, she didn't give a damn about decency because the things she wanted to do with him had no decorum and everything to do with impropriety.

Something fun and "messy," she thought. He'd inserted that word into her brain. That word wanted attention, and she was going to give it the attention it deserved.

<h1 style="text-align:center">FIFTEEN</h1>

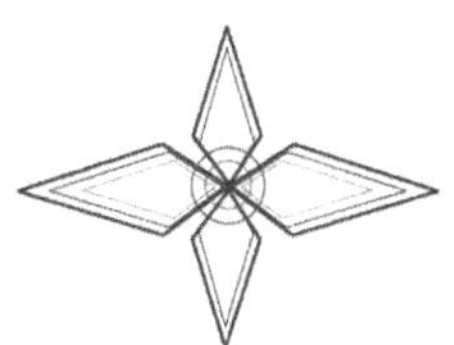

Rita shifted the chair and faced him. The soft light from the single sconce on the wall reflected in his gray eyes, making them appear like two gold stars staring at her. She lifted the hem of his shirt, sliding her fingers under it and over his abdomen.

"Since I'm the Creatress, let's create something unforgettable tonight. I'm good with my hands too." She smiled, and his breath hitched.

"But your back..." His gaze wandered down to where her fingers traced the ripped muscles on his stomach. His body shivered like it was having a private conversation with her fingers.

"I've never felt better. I'm fine. Don't worry."

"Flekken!" He gripped her hand, moved it aside, and took off his shirt, tossing it to the ground. "I want you to see what you do to me."

His body shuddered again as her fingers explored his chest and abdomen, drawing abstract shapes on his green skin. The green darkened, lightened, and darkened as her fingers traveled down to the hem of his pants. His breathing became ragged, matching her own.

Rita didn't know if it was the sweet air from the glistening grass, the sea of stars in the sky, or the abundance of lights from the floral and berry bushes that made her disregard how vulnerable she was in this moment. She was revealing an explorative part of her she hadn't shown to anyone. Even when she was dating Philip, she'd held it back without understanding why. Maybe she'd been saving that sacred part of her heart and soul for Jarzell.

Teal mist flowed around them like a validation to her thoughts.

This vulnerability allowed her to feel and want. She wanted to love again. Jarzell was her chance at the rebirth she craved. This was her transformation. She chose this moment to burst through the door that had kept her safe. Safety wasn't a bad thing; it was a needed space for healing to take place. But now, she was ready to leap into an undiscovered future with sparkling promises, where there was no safety net, and she was okay with that.

Jarzell knew her scars and her history, and he welcomed them. That was what opened her up to him. She could give them a chance at happiness; carving herself a fresh path filled with love and promises of a bright future. There were no guarantees in life. She had to take what she wanted, because life could change instantly. She'd learned to listen to her heart and shut down her mind when creating art. Right now, her heart wanted Jarzell. She wanted to create something sacred with him tonight.

"Are you sure you want this, Rita? Because if you keep touching me like this, I won't be able to stop myself from resisting you." He gritted his teeth.

She smiled, knowing the power she held. "What if I told you I don't want you to resist me?" She pressed her palms into his firm abdomen, one muscle at a time, and her finger ran up and down the center aisle, that defined each side of this stomach. "What if I want you to take me, however and wherever you want? What if I want you to do all kinds of improper things to me?"

This boldness in her fired up her blood.

He cursed as his eyes darkened, and his skin created patterns she hadn't seen before. "Woman, you're making my body feel things I've never felt before. Look at my skin. It's become its own world."

"That's sacred art." She loved how she could affect him like this. He gasped when her palm clamped over his bulge. He throbbed against her grip like a heartbeat pounding for release. The yearning pulsed and pulsed until his hard rod of desire aimed at her.

"I want you." Rita's voice came out low and seductive. The seduction surprised and elated her. This was the passion she'd dreamed of; the kind filled with excitement, fun, and pleasure. "I want to do wild things to you."

In a swift move, he shoved off his pants and underwear, dropping them on the floor. "Do it. Show me your wild side." He begged like a desperate animal.

Rita stared at his green erection, standing tall and proud like a monument that demanded attention. A scar ran down the length of him. Was this the wound that embarrassed him earlier? Her stomach twisted at the excruciating pain he must've experienced.

"What happened here? Does it hurt?"

"A battle wound. A stray blast that I didn't dodge in time. Grandma Ova healed me. It doesn't hurt anymore."

With her finger, she traced the scar, and he twitched. She clasped her fingers around him, wanting to rub away any pain he'd experienced. He moaned as he leaned back against the chair. His knuckles paled as he tightened his grip around the arms of the chair.

She sensed the heat radiating from his body, and that activated the fire inside her. He swallowed, and the veins on his neck swelled with need. His erection grew in her hand, and she wanted to see all of him. She released her grip and got up from her chair.

He let out a disapproving sound. "No... where are you going?"

Rita laughed as she shoved her chair away and kneeled in front of him. She shoved his knees apart. "Going nowhere. I'm just getting myself comfortable for an artistic endeavor."

Desire darkened in his eyes. "Oh yeah? What kind of artist are you?"

"The kind that involves a wild imagination; a close examination. I was an art teacher for a while, so I've acquired a lot of skills. Would you like me to show you?"

"Please do." He opened his legs wider, allowing her the freedom to do whatever she pleased. "Please hurry."

She smiled at his plea, pressing a kiss to the scar that gave him more character. Like hers, his scar wasn't a flaw. It made him unique.

"All better." She took her time kissing his length, hoping he understood how perfect he was. She watched as impatience warred on his face, digging lines into his forehead. She prayed she wouldn't go to hell for this extended ordeal, but she wanted to show him that a little patience could benefit him.

"There are certain things that can't be rushed, *shouldn't* be rushed. Let me 'delegate' the tasks so you can relax, Delegator."

He crooned. "You're so wicked..."

She recalled him offering his services to her when they were in the Crystalline SiSTARS Café.

"You're gorgeous, and you should be on a painting." Rita loved feeling his arousal throb in her hand.

"D-do whatever you want. I don't care." Desperation laced his words. "I just want your mouth on me. You're going to kill me, Rita. You don't know what you're doing…"

"But I *do* know. I know you like this." She bent down and kissed him, and his erection jerked in her grip.

She made him hers with her mouth. *Hers.* Where did that thought come from? It didn't matter because it was the truth. She wanted him to be hers.

"I call this priming the canvas." Her tongue teased him, and his gaze drilled into her. This courageous act startled her, but it also liberated her. His body tensed as if waiting for her next act. This impatient man clung to his sanity but with every kiss she tempted his resolve. She dragged the sexual tension on and on. "The priming is the foreplay. The art comes after."

Rita didn't know she'd be using her artistic skills in this sexual way. That was what she liked about creativity. It came spontaneously. Art was like bacon; it made everything better.

"Paint me all you want. I *love* your painting style. If this is just part of your artistic skill, I want to experience it all." Jarzell gripped the handle of the chair with one hand, and with the other, he caressed her face. "You're my sexy goddess."

No one had ever called her a goddess before. She felt powerful, seeing him come apart before her eyes. "Goddess Rita at your service."

She showed him her artistry with tongue, teeth, and lips. The way his face contorted showed his control was teetering on the edge of passion and release. His moans became a soundtrack that blended with the crickets and the other insects of the night.

Jarzell stiffened and caressed her cheek. "For my first-time with you, I want to release myself inside of you."

He lifted her onto his lap. "That was the most spectacular

art show I've ever experienced. My turn. I *know* what you're doing to my sense of urgency. Now, it's my turn to show you that impatience and patience can be playful toys in lovemaking."

This star-being could see through her intentions, and yet, he played along. "You got me with 'playful toys.' I'm intrigued," she said.

SIXTEEN

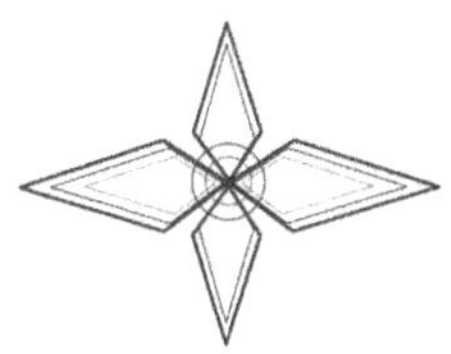

THE TEAL MIST seemed fascinated too because more flowed around them. Simultaneously, streams of smoke emerged from the pores of her skin like heavenly wisps. The two vapors cocooned Jarzell and Rita in their passion for each other. A few floated around like party streamers.

Were these vapors sensing their sexual energy? Or were they merely a swift reaction of their bodies producing "love" vapors? Rita wasn't sure, but her curious mind searched for a logical answer to explain this phenomenon.

"We have company." She waved a hand through the smoke and mist. The two entities snaked around each other, joining as one.

"I don't care. Nothing is stopping me from having you." He removed her top, revealing her braless state. She shivered from the night breeze.

"Show me what you mean by 'playful toys.'" Her nipples hardened, aching for his touch.

He teased them with his fingers, sending heat shooting from her core to every corner of her body. Two kinds of heat bloomed in her; sexual heat and the "magical" heat that couldn't be detected. She didn't know how she could tell the difference between them, but she did.

Both were intense, and that intensity increased as Jarzell's hands and mouth adored her breasts with lazy kisses that made her moan and arch toward him. The unique musky scent of him wrapped around her like seductive arms, and she surrendered to him. His hands caressed the scar that she could hardly feel anymore. His fingers moved patiently around her back, making love to her scar.

With his every touch, her body shivered and sighed as if he was healing her. He pressed his face to her chest and cruised his lips over the curves and dips of her body. The patience he showed brought her body to life. The teal mist and the smoke joined in the air as if they were also making love.

Rita threaded her fingers in his brown hair and studied him as he loved her. She arched a little, shifted a little, offering him all sides of her. When was the last time a man had cherished her like this? He dragged his mouth up to meet hers, kissing her long, slow, and deep.

Jarzell veered back, looking at her. Desperation darkened his eyes. "This is the kind of urgency you spark in me." His mouth crushed down on hers again, and his tongue became the impatient toy that warred with hers. They dueled in her mouth, sending shock waves of pleasure zipping through her body. He angled his mouth, deepening the kiss that drew out a loud, animalistic growl from her.

Did she really sound like that?

He smiled against her mouth. "You're so flekken splendid." He tugged at her pants. "Off with the bottoms."

Rita got up from his lap and gave him permission to remove the last items of clothing. She stood naked in front of him. His gaze burned every inch of her body. Her skin tingled as though her cells vibrated. He got up from his chair and walked around her bare body. Standing behind her, he pulled her against his chest and cupped her breasts. The warmth of him embraced her body. One hand moved to her center, and two fingers entered, thrusting with impatience.

His mouth nibbled her neck. "Are you enjoying this, Rita?"

The muscles in her belly quivered. "Yes."

"Do you want more?" His fingers moved faster, deeper.

Sensations heightened in her system as liquid fire pooled at her core. "Yes."

He nudged her forward. "Bend over the chair, Goddess Rita. I have skills to show you."

She loved the nicknames he gave her from Creatress to Goddess. Each one served a unique purpose filling her with power.

Rita bent over with her hands gripping the arms of the chair. With an arched back, her butt was in the air, fully exposed and at his mercy. Shit, it was hot. She turned, trying to see him.

When his lips pressed to her back, kissing her scar, she closed her eyes and fell into the beauty of his tenderness. Tears welled in her eyes as each kiss wiped away the pain that had lived in her wounds all these years. Her body shuddered from the release of it, and joy replaced the pain.

In that moment, her heart tumbled all the way into his arms. That was where her heart wanted to be, and it frightened her to know it with certainty.

"You're beautiful in every way. This is your personal landscape, Rita. This is your canvas, and I'm going to make it mine too." His tongue traced the length of her scars. He marked her without marking her. He healed her without even knowing.

She surrendered to him wholeheartedly. While his mouth treasured her neck and back, his hands roamed her buttocks. His mouth moved down her spine, igniting a fiery trail that made her body yearn for more. She sensed him closer to her ass and stiffened. Anticipation whirled in her as he gripped her hips, pressing his face into her behind and loving her in every aspect.

Rita gasped at the shock of it. She'd never experienced this before. Streaks of pleasure zigzagged through her, making her feel more alive than ever.

He growled like a wild animal had just been unleashed. Need spiked in her, and she wanted to see him. But all she could do was feel. Waves of bliss knocked her from side to side. Part of her wanted to escape this onslaught of pleasure to breathe, a moment to appreciate the beauty of it. But another part of her wanted more of his overwhelming mouth.

"I want you inside me, right now." Rita breathed. "Right now." Desperation pulled at her.

He laughed with a throaty purr of approval. "Who's impatient now?"

She didn't care. She needed to feel him inside her. She wanted that connection. "I want you."

Jarzell pressed his arousal against her buttocks and whispered, "I don't have any Safe-Sex Spray with me."

"It's okay. I'm taking a contraceptive herb. I'm good."

"Just so you know, I'm clean."

"Me too." She arched her back even further. "Hurry."

He laughed again. "I like this impatient side of you. Especially when I'm the reason."

"Stop talking." Desire whirled in her body. "You're going to send me flying before you're even inside me."

In one swift move, he plunged into her. She gasped as her muscles stretched and stretched to accommodate him. Her body quivered with delight. He crooned as he thrust into her, increasing his speed. Stars sparkled in her vision, and heat radiated from where they joined.

He lowered himself against her sweat-slicked back and

plunged like a warrior fighting for his life. Pleasure ricocheted down his body, reverberating against hers. His ecstasy roared into the night, and somewhere, an owl hooted in agreement.

He growled into her ear. "You're mine, Rita."

"You're mine too," she whispered back.

The sweet air around them took on a new aroma; one that was filled with sweat, sex, love, and hope.

Jarzell remained inside her while his fingers found their union. "I want this every night with you." His warm breath caressed her ear. She whimpered as he moved again, taking her higher and higher. "That's right. I want to feel your release."

Rita couldn't hold on any longer and leaped off the most exquisite cliff, sobbing out his name.

While her heavy breathing calmed, Jarzell gathered her into his arms. He carried her into the bedroom, placing her down on the bed as though she was a delicate treasure. He got her a towel to clean herself while he returned to the bathroom and washed himself. Grandma Ova had a drawer full of clothing that accommodated several sizes for her guests. Rita changed into clean underwear and a new set of pajamas. She left one on the bed for Jarzell.

"Thanks, but I'll only need the pants. I'm still burning up from our escapade."

Tingles zipped across her body from his gaze. She couldn't believe what they had done outside on the deck. "I hope Grandma Ova didn't hear us."

"Even if she did, I'm sure she wouldn't care. There's nothing wrong with two people loving each other."

"Yeah, but this is *her home.*"

"And we did it on the private deck of the guest room. It's not like we dishonored her bedroom."

True, but still.

"Well, if it makes you feel better, we can recreate the love scenes at my place. We can do it in every room in my house. With your creative mind and my willingness to let you do whatever you want to me, we'll have the most creative ways to have sex." A wide grin splashed on his face.

She liked the idea more than she realized, but she didn't reply. She was still deciding on the invitation. She got into bed, expecting him to go to his own guest room.

Instead, Jarzell slid into bed with her. "I'm sleeping here tonight, if you don't mind."

She stared at him. The idea of him sleeping beside her was more intimate than the sex they just had. This intimacy meant things were becoming *more*. That it wasn't just sex.

Was she ready for more?

"Is it okay?" he asked when she didn't reply. "I want to make sure you don't have any nightmares from the event today." He brushed the hair away from her forehead.

The genuine concern settled the nerves in her stomach. When was the last time she had a man sleeping in her bed? It had been too long. Heat ran down her arm as if it wanted her to say yes.

"Yeah, that's okay."

Jarzell fell asleep before Rita. She stayed awake, reliving the events of the day. So much had happened in a brief span of time that she needed to understand it all. Most of all, she wanted to comprehend where this relationship was going. Just because she had fallen for him didn't mean she stopped being cautious. If anything, she was more careful now because she was most vulnerable now.

Her eyes became heavy, and she was about to fall asleep when a stream of teal mist emerged from Jarzell and moved in front of her. As the teal mist and her white smoke merged, it became a beautiful aqua or light teal vapor. The vapor took on various abstract shapes. But as an artist, her imagination saw faces of animals and strange beings. Some faces had feline or wolfish eyes, while others depicted protruding eyes. She caught images of big and small ears, short hair, and long hair. The facial features moved fluidly with the vapors. It was difficult to grasp onto the details.

Why were the teal mist and the white smoke showing her this? What did they want her to know?

Her heart lurched with excitement when an idea popped into her mind. Were they giving her clues on where the Sacred Tablet could be? Or were they telling her how to protect Saedo?

She fell asleep with a list of questions to ask Grandma Ova in the morning.

<h1 style="text-align:center">SEVENTEEN</h1>

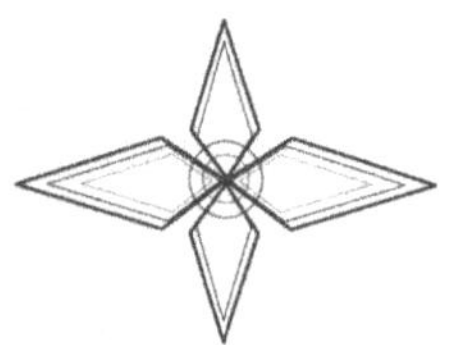

Rita woke to voices from outside the window. To her surprise, her back showed no indication of discomfort. In fact, her body felt rejuvenated. She glanced at her bracelet. It was nine thirty in the morning. She'd overslept! She had never overslept before. She shot up in bed and looked over to the empty spot where Jarzell had lain.

Why didn't he wake her? They had things to do today.

She rushed into the bathroom and washed up with cool water that freshened her face. A little soreness bloomed between her thighs, and she smiled at the memory from last night. She noticed a new set of clothes folded on the counter beside stacks of towels: a light-weight cotton top and a pair of Ingavex pants from her sister's fashion collection. The materials of the pants induced the metabolism in her buttocks, thighs, and calves. She peeked at the sizes on the clothes and smiled that they were correct.

Did Jarzell get these for her? Or was it Grandma Ova? She had planned on making a trip back to her apartment to change before returning here for questions. But this thoughtfulness saved her a trip.

After changing into the new clothes, she went out to the garden. The smell of coffee snuck up her nose, and her body jolted from recognizing the energy booster. Saedo had delicious coffee that grew from some vine that magically appeared on a rock. They harvested the bean and now there was a vast farm with acres of coffee plants. This produce was one of the best products that were exported to neighboring regions and galaxies.

Rita was used to Saedo coffee, which possessed a variety of strong flavors that could be enhanced with floral cream or plant-based milk. But there was something different about this aroma that had her body relaxing in inexplicable ways.

She found Jarzell and Grandma Ova in a garden full of lush bushes and flowers. Grandma Ova wore a sun hat with energy swirling around the rim like it was collecting solar energy. White hair peeked out from the sides. Jarzell held a shovel device that created a hole in the ground faster than a regular shovel she was used to seeing on Earth.

"That's good enough," said Grandma Ova, clapping dirt off her hands. "Put the tree in there and cover it up. I'll water it later." She glanced up at Rita. "There you are. How are you feeling? Do you want some coffee? It's my new recipe."

"Sure." She met Jarzell's warm gaze. "Thanks for the clothes. When did you get them? They fit nicely."

"I placed an order with Stellium Couture before we went to bed. I found your size from your bloodstained clothing. I figured you would need something to wear and so did I. The droids dropped the orders off early this morning."

Not only was he efficient, he was also resourceful. This was one of those moments when she didn't mind his sense of urgency. The perfect timing gave her the clothes and saved her time. "Thank you."

"You're welcome." Jarzell leaned in and the scent of citrus

aftershave made her want to pull him in closer. "It's the least I can do for the best night I've ever experienced." He flashed her a wicked grin as he dragged over a small tree and dropped it into the hole. "I just need to plant this coffee tree for Grandma Ova. I'll catch up with you."

Rita nodded, returning the warm smile. As she fell into step with Grandma Ova, she remembered how his body had felt against hers during sleep. She wanted that intimacy again, that warmth that made her feel safe.

"My garden assistants can't come until later, so Jarzell offered to help." Grandma Ova took off her hat. "That's enough scalp massage today."

"Is that what it was doing?" Rita studied the innovative sun hat.

"Yup. The hat massages my scalp, allowing good blood flow to my head. This will ensure I won't have any hair-loss problem."

The full head of white hair with the classic haircut from Sasha was proof that, at her age of one thousand and three hundred solar cycles, Grandma Ova still looked like someone who was only in her sixties. Rita remembered reading that time and energy on this planet differed from Earth, and here was the living example.

"You have more hair than me." Rita threaded her fingers through her hair, where hints of the natural brown glistened against the fading purple.

"Feel free to use this scalp-massager if you'd like."

"Thanks, but I can get one in the Village Center."

Grandma Ova strode by a bush with large flowers the size of her palms. They dangled like vases hanging from thick vines. They reminded her of the pitcher plant on Earth, but these were white, and they had intricate designs on the surface. Grandma Ova placed her hands near one, and the vase tipped, pouring water onto her hands as she washed dirt from them.

Rita hadn't seen it around Saedo. "What kind of plant is this?"

"It's one of our rain collecting plants. This one is a white vazzlette. Take a look." Grandma Ova held one up for Rita. Inside, water filled it like a well. "When it rains, the 'vase' flower collects water and saves it for sunny days when there's no rain. The roots can detect how dry the soil is and disperse the water when needed. The roots can distribute water to other plants around it too. These vazzlettes have long, deep roots, so they're very helpful."

"That's amazing." The plant life in Saedo astounded and fascinated her. She discovered something new every day.

Two little felicitees that looked like goldfinches with six wings landed on the vazzlette and began drinking from the mouth. After the birds drank, they sang a beautiful song that melted Rita's anxiety. She had a to-do list weighing on her mind when she woke. But these adorable birds removed that stress. So much joy emanated from their song. Even the vazzlettes swayed back and forth like they were dancing.

Rita followed Grandma Ova over to a large deck with potted plants. They sat at a round table. Grandma Ova poured a cup of blue coffee for Rita. "This is a new hybrid coffee bean I just created. Try it and let me know what you think."

"Thank you." Rita sipped and sighed. "It's heavenly." She savored the unique flavor. "There's a subtle sweet taste to it. Did you add any sugar or honey to it?"

"Nothing, it's all natural. I cross pollinated the blue sugarcane with the coffee plant. These two species don't normally go together, but science and the natural world allow magical possibilities to emerge. All it takes is a little creativity. As long as you are using this method in ways that help the land and others, it's a good thing. I needed a different coffee that's naturally sweet—but not too sweet—that can help regulate the glucose levels in my blood."

Rita placed her cup down. "Really? This drink helps regulate your glucose?"

Grandma Ova beamed and gestured to her abundant garden "Yes. We have all the resources we need for food and good health. We just need to find it. The trick is in the finding. Everything takes time and effort. Saedo's land is fertile with possibilities." Amber eyes connected with Rita. "Earth is too. I think sometimes humans forget that. But there are a few humans who understand this magic—this gift—and are connecting to the natural world now. I can sense it." She clasped her hands together, looking at Rita. "Anyway, we aren't here to talk about my plants or my glucose or cholesterol levels."

Rita tried to imagine what Earth would be like if people started focusing on finding the remedies hidden in nature. Would human health and longevity improve? Probably. But who would take that initiative?

She wasn't living on Earth any longer; she was in Saedo. And right now, this land was her home, and her home was in danger. It was odd how she woke with a list of things to do and questions for Grandma Ova, but the felicitees and the lush garden lessened the urgency, allowing her to think clearly.

"I have some questions I need your help with."

"I'll do my best to answer them."

Jarzell approached after cleansing his hands from the vazzlettes. "Your coffee tree is all set. It's heavier than it looks."

"Thanks for your help."

Jarzell pulled out a chair beside Rita, sat, and took the cup of coffee Grandma Ova offered. Teal mist flowed around him.

"Where should we start?" Grandma Ova asked.

"How about: what's the significance of teal mist joining with smoke?"

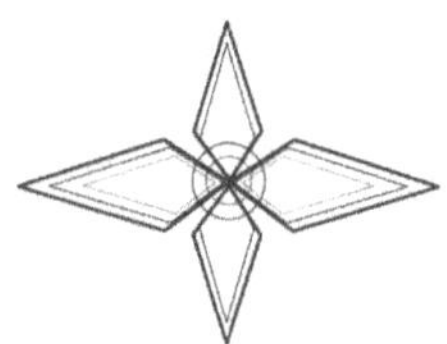

EIGHTEEN

Grandma Ova's mouth dropped open. "What did you say?"

"I see the teal mist from Jarzell joining with a white smoke that comes from me."

Grandma Ova tented her hands in a thinking manner. "First, I want to know if you've found any clues regarding the location of the Sacred Tablet."

Rita and Jarzell shook their heads. "Not yet."

"Okay. It's making more sense now," she said, almost muttering to herself.

"The tablet isn't visible for a reason, and the mist and the smoke are clues to find it."

Rita furrowed her eyebrows. "How so?"

"First off, I have to share something that many citizens don't know about." She looked over at Jarzell. "There are three Sacred Tablets. Besides me, Chief Mozar and few members of the government know this. The tablets were made from the brown Saedonite crystal. This rare stone went through an alchemical process that makes it look like glass. But it's a natural stone, not engineered by star-beings or any machines. The other two are placed in safe areas in Saedo."

Jarzell and Rita exchanged an inquisitive glance.

"Are they missing too?" Rita asked the first question that popped into her mind.

"No, they're fine."

"Where are they?" Jarzell inquired.

"One is at a tattoo parlor, the other is in a museum. They're in places that are 'safe,' according to them." Grandma Ova met Rita's curious eyes. "I've read what's on the tablets, and they prefer to be presentable and accessible. No one can access their information if they don't want it revealed. These tablets give off a healing energy from the Saedonite crystal. So it was best to leave them open in Saedo for everyone to benefit from."

Jarzell finished his coffee. "What's on the missing tablet? Can you share the information?"

"These tablets contain the wisdom of Saedo: a collection of stories, codes, magical spells that have been used for eons. They're like a blueprint, an evolution map of this land and its potential growth."

Rita had a feeling Grandma Ova was more involved with these tablets than just someone who saw the information. "How do you know these things?"

Grandma Ova's eyes sparked. "I'm part of the Ancestral Council. Most of them have passed on to the other side of the veil. I'm here, and I'll do my best to ensure Saedo thrives."

Jarzell turned to Grandma Ova. "I've never heard of the council. Do the villagers know this about you?"

"Not many, and I want to keep it that way. Certain things are safer when they're not broadcasted. The Ancestral Council works with other realms. There's no need for everyone to know or question because things like that are difficult to explain and comprehend. I want to keep things simple for the villagers. Sometimes too much information will backfire." She smiled at Jarzell and Rita. "You're here to find the missing tablet. I'll help you as much as I can. Even though I'm part of the council, I don't know everything. No one knows everything."

Rita had more questions about Grandma Ova, but she didn't want to pry. "Why did you separate the tablets?"

"If we placed them all in one place; that would be like putting all the eggs into one basket and inviting enemies to come and steal them. We placed one in the Village Library, a place where the public could view it. The library is filled with other special books, so a glass tablet is just one of many special things on display."

Two felicitees flew onto the ledge of the deck, and Grandma Ova got up and poured seeds into a feeder for them.

"These books are their own spirit. They have their own consciousness. They have their own agenda. If they sense danger, they can make themselves invisible; go to places where they can't be found. This is why it was okay to display them in a public area. But in this case, one went missing because it needed to connect the two of you. That's my educated guess."

"Why?" Jarzell shared the same bafflement as Rita.

Grandma Ova sat back down and turned to Rita. "You see Jarzell's teal mist. You know what that means, right?" Her gaze slid over to Jarzell.

"We do," Jarzell said. "I had feelings for her from the beginning, before the tablet went missing."

"You came to the library *because* the Sacred Tablet went missing," Rita said.

Jarzell clasped her hand. "I would've come to see you sooner or later, but yes, the case was a priority for Chief Mozar."

"Fate is a marvel. We can't avoid it, nor should we try. Just work with it. There's a reason things happen the way they do. If you try to dissect it too much, it's not 'pretty' anymore, it becomes a project, you know what I mean?"

Rita let out a sigh. "I know. I've asked myself too many questions about these sudden and powerful feelings. But I can't come to a clear answer. The only thing that makes sense is my feelings."

"Exactly." Grandma Ova snapped her fingers. "You hit the nail on the head, Rita. Certain things aren't mental. They stem from a deep place; a place that's in between, where only emotion can get to. Anyway, the union of the teal mist and the smoke is symbolic of the two of you."

"I find it very odd that smoke can surface from my body." Rita recalled the video that Jarzell had shown her.

"It's a rare phenomenon. Heat is usually associated with smoke. Did you feel sudden heat in your body?"

"Yes! What does that mean?" Rita's eyes beamed. Finally, she could get some answers.

"We all have a past that makes us who we are. Some pasts are darker than others. Remember, everything is energy. The pain you went through *calcified* in your body, hiding in your bones, between your organs, glands, and psyche. Your body's way of decalcification is heat. The heat melted or 'broke away' that calcification, and the smoke released it through your pores."

Every word from Grandma Ova made sense. The energy in Saedo probably expedited Rita's healing.

A concern bothered her. "So does that mean the smoke is poisonous?"

Grandma Ova shook her head. "The 'negative' energy was broken down during the process. The poison that was collected with the healing leaf came from the Ulkrin hybrid."

Now Rita understood why she was able to connect to her joy, creativity, and desire again. There was nothing holding her back.

"I've never seen the healing process happen on a human body," Grandma Ova said. "I've encountered humans before you and your sisters arrived in Saedo, but none of them possessed the vibrant energy that you give off. I sensed the love you have for one another, including the love you're capable of offering to your starmate. Each of you possess a rare energy—a special gift—that speaks to Saedo land." She folded her hands on the table.

"It appears Saedo is in a transitional mode and needs all the assistance it can get," Jarzell said.

"That's the reason you and your sisters are here." Grandma Ova eyed Rita. "You're in Saedo because you're connected to someone here." Her attention swerved to Jarzell. "That union births a *new* energy, and that energy will not only help protect this land, it will also push Saedo to a higher frequency. That means more healing, more inventions, more plant life, cleaner air, and so on. The possibilities are endless. But as Saedo becomes a gem, enemies will come too." She rose up from the chair, walked around her deck, picked off dried leaves from the potted plants, and glanced out into the yard at nothing in particular.

Grandma Ova's contemplative mood was a contrast to her usually carefree attitude, which meant something worried her.

Jarzell waved a hand through the teal mist and the white smoke.

Grandma Ova strode back to the table. "What color does the teal mist and smoke make?"

"Aqua." Rita held up a hand as a serpent stream of smoke snaked around her wrist, and the scent of cedar warmed her.

"That could be a clue to the location of the Sacred Tablet," Grandma Ova said.

Jarzell pulled out a screen from his wristband that showed an organized chart of information he'd collected. He added the aqua detail, pressed a button, and shared it with Rita's bracelet.

"Remember, you're living on a different planet now. The energy here isn't the same as that on Earth. Your body and your mind can now register and respond to higher frequencies. You can't ignore them; they want your attention for a reason. It's natural to sense things. We're all born with intuition. Here in Saedo, your human body's sensitivity is heightened."

Rita's lips twisted. "I'm not ignoring them. I want to understand them."

"Good." Grandma Ova sniffed and smiled. "Ah, what a lovely scent. The cedrus tree resonates with you. This is amazing, Rita. You don't know what this means. The Saedo cedrus is a sacred tree. Its healing abilities are endless. What's more, it has the ability to ward off darkness. I want to show both of you something. Come with me."

Jarzell and Rita followed Grandma Ova down the deck. Rita was grateful for all the information Grandma Ova gave her. Now she could make some sense of how the mist, smoke, and cedrus scent were all connected.

Rita recalled the smoke coming from her pores. Any normal person would be frightened, but she wasn't. She'd always been different. Maybe it was her shyness that made her retreat into herself as a young girl. She'd wondered about life beyond Earth, life beyond Pluto. She'd sit in her yard and talk to the trees. The trees didn't judge. They listened and became her friends.

You're so weird. Her sisters used to call her weird, strange, and odd, but not condescendingly. They knew her character and had left her to do what she wanted. Each of her siblings had a unique aspect to them. Didn't everyone? And it was difficult for Rita to find friends and keep them. The same with men.

What does Jarzell like about her? Would he stay with her forever?

No one truly knew the length of "forever." These star-beings lived longer lives. Would her life adjust to this longevity? Self-doubts had a way of sneaking into her thoughts. She kicked them away without hesitation.

Grandma Ova took them to an extensive garden. As they rounded the corner, Jarzell's gray eyes met Rita's, and she shivered, remembering last night's event. It was the sexiest evening she'd ever had with a man; in this case, a star-being. It was also her first-time making love outdoors. With all the crucial information she just received from Grandma Ova, it didn't affect Rita's body's reaction to him one bit. It seemed like nothing could stand between them.

Grandma Ova gestured to the four stone seats that surrounded a fire pit composed of the same dark gray stones covered in burned markings.

Rita sat down on the stone. The warmth surprised her, but it was probably from the heat of the suns.

Grandma placed some logs into the pit. "It's time you get a brief lesson on mist and smoke. It'll help you comprehend the magnitude of what's happening."

"I'm ready for that," Rita said.

"Maybe it'll answer some questions for me too," Jarzell muttered while he started the fire with the lighter. The statement was casual and low. Rita didn't think Grandma Ova heard him. If she did, she didn't show any signs of it.

What kinds of questions did he have?

With a long stick, Grandma Ova dispersed the fire and smoke emerged. Rita recognized the scent immediately.

"This is Saedo cedrus wood," Grandma Ova said. "Look at the smoke. What do you see?"

Rita glanced at the smoke and watched it move like a slow dance in the air. The teal mist stayed back, hanging around her feet and Jarzell's legs. It was as if the teal mist was watching and waiting too. "I see smoke. Moving streams of it."

"Me too." Jarzell shrugged. "Am I supposed to see something else?"

"It's normal to see the smoke for what it is," Grandma Ova

said. "Smoke is a dry vapor, and mist is a wet vapor. We are working with elements here, water and fire. Smoke comes from fire, and mist comes from moisture, hence water." She poked at the fire pit and a flame burst at the center.

The flame turned blue, and Rita whipped her head at Jarzell. "Do you see the blue flame?"

Jarzell nodded, and Grandma Ova smiled. "It's the fire giving you a message. Let's pay attention."

Smoke from the blue flame surfaced in slow movements that took on various shapes. Trees, flowers, symbols, and some words in the universal text. Three words lingered longer than the others: *a love story*.

What did that mean? Rita's eyes widened when the streams of smoke appeared to dance in front of her.

Dancing for her.

She glanced at Grandma Ova and Jarzell to see if they witnessed the same occurrence or if it was just her imagination.

"Why is the smoke hovering around you?" Jarzell tried blowing at it, but it didn't move where he blew. It stayed in place.

Grandma Ova's eyes brightened and placed a hand over her chest. "This image delights my corra."

The smoke formed an abstract pattern Rita didn't recognize.

"Do you see the magic of smoke and mist?" Grandma Ova gazed at the fluctuating vapors.

Unsure of what she meant, Rita and Jarzell shook their heads.

"If you study the smoke, the way it moves, you'll notice that after a while it just disappears. Where does it go? It only vanishes from *your* perspective. But in reality, it travels to an unseen world, carrying messages, medicine, codes, and other things. Basically, smoke can maneuver between the seen and unseen worlds."

Rita's body warmed from Grandma Ova's explanation. "That explains why the body-reader couldn't register the strange heat in my body. The heat was from a different dimension..."

Jarzell looked at Rita. "I just realized something interesting. The healed scars on your back look like streams of smoke." He gestured to the smoke slithering around their feet.

Grandma Ova turned to Rita. "A lot of the scars disappeared yesterday. Is it okay if I look at your scars once more?"

Jarzell's wristband buzzed. He glanced down and rose from his seat. "I need to take this call. I'll be back." He strode off.

"Yes, please look." Rita turned, giving Grandma Ova access to her back.

Grandma Ova held up the hem of her shirt. "It is similar to a stream of smoke. There are no coincidences, my darling. Let me show you." A virtual screen splashed in front of Rita. "This proves that the Cosmos works in odd and unpredictable ways."

Rita straightened her shirt and stared at the small S-shaped image. The other scars had disappeared. "All of this makes me think the smoke is intelligent. It was there when I gained my scars, and now it adjusted itself because *I'm* adjusting to my new life."

Grandma Ova nodded. "Like I said, smoke is its own being. It can travel through several dimensions. Fire creates smoke. So maybe this particular dry vapor was present the day of your car accident. Maybe it assisted you in some way. Maybe it picked up on your energy and knew that you were needed in Saedo. There are so many 'maybes' and we can sit here all day discussing the possibilities. But the truth of the matter is that you're meant to be here."

"And to be with Jarzell." Rita's heart galloped. She stared up at the bright blue sky and realized she'd never comprehend the web of interconnectedness that created the Universe.

Grandma Ova stared at her. "I've met some of your sisters. When Vanessa first saw Arkon's mist, she didn't know how to feel or act either. She was afraid, insecure about her feelings. Was it fate or was it her corra's true reaction? But in the end, she figured it out."

Rita hadn't had time to sit down with her sisters for a heart-to-heart conversation yet. She made a mental note to schedule another sisters' gathering soon since she had missed the last one at Sasha's house.

"When Jarzell and his brothers rescued me and my sisters, I noticed him. How could a girl not notice him, right?"

Grandma Ova laughed. "If I was younger, I'd be the first in line to ask him on a date. Those muscles would make any female twitch in several places."

Rita burst into laughter. "Do you have a starmate?"

Nodding, Grandma Ova smiled. "That's a story for another time, darling. Today is *your* story."

Rita had never imagined having a sexual discussion with someone over a thousand solar cycles old. But this casual chat lightened the seriousness of everything else. She held onto that ease for a bit longer.

"But I never made a move or anything," Rita said. "I was still working on healing myself from a previous relationship."

"Who hurt you?" Grandma Ova's eyes hardened like an overprotective parent.

Rita released a sigh and told her story. "It took a long time for me to understand that my scars aren't a reflection of me. I know better now. My scars aren't flaws; they're symbols of strength. They remind me of my survival."

"Good." Grandma Ova clasped her hands over Rita's. "Loving energy radiates from you. That beauty comes from self-love. I can sense that it's a new frequency, one that you've just welcomed into your life." Her amber eyes beamed. "No matter what you've experienced prior to this moment, your ability to accept yourself is the beginning of a miraculous journey. It allows you to love a star-being who is fated to you. Whether or not you accept him, that's still your choice. You have free will, no matter what the lore is. Fate is an interesting topic. It follows you as you learn and take detours from the main path. But eventually, all rivers lead to the ocean. You'll end up where you're meant to be."

"I know. I feel strongly about Jarzell. The more time I spend with him, the more I feel for him. That scares me because I've never felt this way about anyone, and I wonder if it's going too fast."

Grandma Ova tapped her own chest. "Just quiet your mind and listen to your corra. It doesn't lie. Magic and miracles happen every day. Sometimes we dismiss them. You've been given a gift, Rita. What you do with it is up to you."

This conversation with someone wiser than Rita helped her see to the core of her issue. She remembered the wish she had tossed out to the Universe on that fateful New Year's Eve night. *I deserve a man who loves me for my wounds and for all I aspire to be.*

When she made that wish, she didn't know if there was such a man. Why would a man want a flawed person such as herself? But here was Jarzell, who not only saw her scars, he kissed them, loved them. How could she not accept someone like that?

"You're right. It's up to me what I do with my gift. Thank you for helping me with… everything."

Grandma Ova released Rita's hand. "I was young once. Love is a complicated and beautiful thing. The lessons I learned are that you *have* to have fun. Laughter and spontaneity always make a relationship more interesting. Especially the sex, you know."

Rita's shoulders shook from laughter. She couldn't believe Grandma Ova was giving her sexual advice. This must be why her siblings enjoyed talking to this wise star-being who knew so much about everything.

Rita's imagination piqued. "There's something I want to ask you. I used to paint a lot. I'm ready to paint again. What kinds of paint are available in Saedo?"

"That depends. Are you referring to a medium for paper, canvas, wood, metal, or stone?" Her eyebrows wiggled. "Or are you referring to something that can be layered onto *skin*?"

Did Grandma's voice just purr?

Rita's cheeks burned. "Both?"

"You're in luck. I have some available in my storage."

Rita's eyebrows lifted with surprise. "Why do you have them? Do you paint too?"

"I don't have time anymore. My gardens are my passions now. But I can't resist an art sale. I have a huge closet full of things I'll probably never use. Somehow, I knew they'd be put to good use one day. Spark Your Imagination in the Village Center has a vast variety of paints and other things for your creative needs."

Rita had strode by that store a few times in the past, but she hadn't had the itch to jump into painting until now. She'd have to stop in soon.

Jarzell rushed back with urgency on his face. "I've got to go help my brothers. Raeko, Arkon, and Zeycott are at the scene now. A dark well has just emerged near a public park. Raeko just killed a hybrid Ulkrin beast. More are coming."

"Go," Rita said. "Don't worry about me." She could always call one of her sisters for a ride home or call a carrier to pick her up.

After Jarzell left, Grandma Ova asked, "What does the well look like?"

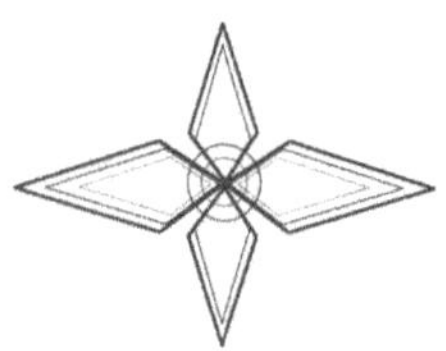

NINETEEN

Rita pictured the dark well in her mind. "It's not small, about three feet in diameter. But there's a whirlpool in the center. How are they able to create portals like this? Can anyone create portals?"

"Everything is energy, and energy can be manipulated," Grandma Ova said. "That's what they did with the storm."

"We must stop them. I mean, how far will they go? What else are they up to?"

A strong cedrus scent snuck up Rita's nose. She followed the aroma to a massive cedrus tree standing on the other side of the garden. Smoke surfaced from its bark. "Do you see the smoke?"

Nodding, Grandma Ova placed a gentle hand on Rita's back. "This wise tree is trying to connect to you. I suggest you sit down tonight and quiet your mind. Open up to it. I can give you some dry cedrus leaves to burn. It'll help clear your mind, opening you up to receive messages. There's one thing I didn't have time to mention to you and Jarzell. Smoke can offer messages through a method called pyromancy, which is the divination of fire and what emits from it. Smoke creates images and symbols that can be interpreted in many ways."

"Sort of like tarot card readings, but with smoke?"

"Exactly." Grandma Ova placed a hand on the bark. "You have a connection with the cedrus. See what it has to show you. The reading is subjective. You're an artist, so you'll see and understand the symbols better than most. Plus, you'll *feel* it. Try it tonight or whenever you have time and let me know what you see. If you need help to decipher the images, send them to my smart pendant." She pulled out a gold circle that dangled from a chain. A light beamed to Rita's bracelet. "I'll do what I can to help."

"Thank you. I'm going to head home now and do some more research." Concern tumbled in Rita's stomach, wondering if Jarzell was safe.

Grandma Ova pulled out a drawer with dried herbs and gathered some into a glass container. She placed it into the same bag that held the paints. "Like any reading, it's a personal experience. Hone into your senses and see what comes up." She handed over the bag. "There's something I'm forgetting. Something's blocking my mind. Maybe it's meant for you to discover. But I feel it has something to do with Jarzell's mist and the scented smoke from you."

"Jarzell mentioned he felt something from Derwood Creek when he battled the squirmurs there."

Grandma twisted her lips. "That's another clue. All I can tell you is to look at the details and trust your intuition."

This visit had turned into something way more than Rita had expected. "Thank you for your guidance and time. I'm going to call a carrier to pick me up."

"Do you want to borrow my personal rider? You can return it the next time you stop by."

Rita appreciated the friendly gesture, but what if Grandma Ova needed to go somewhere? "No, thanks. A carrier will be fine."

Rita asked the carrier to stop at Spark Your Imagination for some state-of-the-art paints. Thirty minutes later, the carrier dropped her off at her home.

Inside her apartment, Rita couldn't sit still; her mind was restless. She checked her bracelet, but didn't see a message from Jarzell, so she sent one.

Is everything all right? Let me know. I'm at home already.

Hopefully, he and his brothers destroyed the dark portal with no one getting hurt.

Rita didn't want to sit around, worrying about something she couldn't control. She took out the tubes of paints that Grandma Ova gave her and set them aside. Her heart thudded with intimate plans with Jarzell. She'd never been this bold with a man before. She wanted him to model for her. She wanted to paint him. He'd be her first painting on this planet. He was the inspiration that pushed her to create again. That deserved something special.

But of course, it had to wait until later. Right now, it seemed like danger lurked everywhere. What if the Ulkrins had other beasts or parasites already hidden here? How could the Saedo villagers protect themselves? It would be difficult to react if a sudden attack occurred in places they weren't expecting—like the public park where Jarzell was at.

Rita sent a message to her siblings. *Everyone safe?*

Vanessa replied, "Yes. *My stomach's been acting up. That means something is about to happen again.*" Her sister had sensed the squirmurs before they attacked her and Arkon.

The other sisters replied that everything was fine, and that they were taking the next few days off to stay inside.

Rita informed her siblings she was safe and at home. When the other sisters clicked off, Vanessa remained. *I'm calling you.*

Vanessa and her long, red hair popped onto her virtual

screen. "Why did you ask that question? Did you sense something too?"

Rita debated on what to share with her sister. She didn't want Vanessa or anyone to worry.

Vanessa always had a sixth sense about things, but on this planet, it was ten times stronger. She could probably read into Rita's half-truths, and that would create more questions.

Rita wasn't in the mood for a lengthy explanation, so she said, "Yes. My body's been acting strange. Sensing more heat than usual."

"You've always been able to sense heat, which we all thought was weird. Do you remember the time Inga was injured playing with matches at her friend's house? You sensed it on your pinkie finger. And Inga got burned on her pinkie."

Rita flipped back to that memory. Goodness, how did she forget that? Maybe she'd shoved a lot of herself away when she'd fallen into her depression.

"Thanks for the reminder. I'd forgotten about that."

"You have a connection to fire or an aspect of it," Vanessa said. "I've been researching on the Galacto Net, and every mist color that has been activated is waking up Saedo."

Rita believed it. "I have something to share with you."

"You saw Jarzell's mist?"

Rita dropped her mouth at Vanessa's sixth sense.

Rita nodded. "Yeah. My emotions are strong. What do I do?"

"Just go with the flow." Vanessa beamed. "You're the fifth sister to see your forever mate's mist color. Every time one of us connects to a star-being, a new frequency is created. That's what Grandma Ova said, and that makes sense. Saedo is becoming more alive with us here. That's probably why the damn Ulkrins want the land. I wonder who's next? Isabella or Nina?"

Rita spent a few more minutes chatting with Vanessa until she said she had to go.

Rita had a quick lunch from the food Emma had given her. Rita checked her bracelet again but didn't see any messages from Jarzell.

Where is he? Why isn't he replying? Doesn't he know she's worried? Why can't he just stop what he's doing to send one message?

Oh God, she needed help. What was wrong with her? Since when did she become an impatient girlfriend? Was she even his girlfriend? They hadn't discussed that or anything about a long-term relationship. Regardless of how attracted she was to him, she needed to know. She didn't want a fling. It didn't matter if she saw his mist or not. If he wasn't interested in a serious relationship, then she'd walk away. She wasn't in the mood for games.

Had he assumed that she assumed they were "together" now because of the mist? Well, he needed to know that female brains thought differently. A woman needed a straightforward answer to settle the scenarios playing in her head.

Heat bloomed from her gut and expanded out to her limbs, pushing all distractions away. It was time to connect to the cedrus tree. Why was it calling her?

She strode to the living room with two dark brown couches and a pale yellow coffee table and settled on the area rug with a large metal plate. She crisscrossed her legs, taking out the dry cedar leaves Grandma Ova had given her. She placed them inside a mini iron cauldron that Grandma Ova had also packed. With a lighter, Rita burned the dried leaves, dropping them into the cauldron. She didn't really know what else to do. She wasn't used to rituals. But the one thing she knew was to speak from the heart. So, she spoke to the fire, smoke, and cedrus.

"I'm here. I'm watching you. I'm listening." The aromatic

scent swirled around the room. "What do you need me to know?"

Rita's eyes widened when a teal flame emerged from the mini cauldron like a blossoming flower. She stared at the flame that couldn't have come from the few tiny cedrus leaves. But magic occurred in inexplicable ways.

Smoke dispersed from the flames. "We're glad you connected to us."

The flames and smoke pulsed from the words. The voice that had a unique echo appeared to be male. She couldn't believe she was talking to fire and smoke. Rita squinted her eyes as the smoke formed abstract images.

"What do you need me to know?"

"Call on fire and smoke to help you. We *need* you to do this when the time comes."

"Why me?"

"Because your energy is the perfect polarity with Jarzell. He has a connection to water. He is the water to your fire. Both of you create a unique vapor that will help protect Saedo. Together, you can go to a place that no one else can go. That place is where the Sacred Tablet is."

Realization dawned on her. Was this what Grandma Ova was trying to clarify, but couldn't? That Jarzell represented the moist vapors and she the dry vapors?

"Where is this place? When do I go? How do I go there?" So many questions shot to the forefront. What if she made a mistake and they failed to find the tablet?

"You'll know. This is your journey."

"Who are you?" Rita asked.

"We're family."

Family? What did that mean?

The smoke circled around her wrists while the teal flame

grew into a bigger flower that took over the room. Fear spiked in her at the potential catastrophe; her home could burn.

"Our flames won't destroy your home."

Relief settled in her. "What do you mean by family?"

"When each of your sisters connected with their starmate, that love frequency pushed Saedo to a higher vibration. You *woke* us up. Consider us as sleeping ancestors of the land. We'd been dormant for a while until this new energy wave opened up new possibilities."

How could a human show these star-beings new possibilities? They were the ones with all the high-tech stuff that blew her mind. They were the intelligent beings with all the magnificent plants and creatures.

"Humans are special." The smoke swirled around her chest, right over her heart. "You just don't believe it. When you do, magic happens. Right now, you're speaking to a flame and smoke. Was that possible before?"

They were right. In the past, Rita had always held back a little of herself because of an emotion or an insecurity that weighed her down. If none of those things had bothered her, would she have soared to success and happiness? She didn't know. What she did know was that she'd found something here worth her time and her heart: Jarzell. Not only that, but she'd also found herself again.

A sudden noise erupted from somewhere. It echoed through the teal flames.

"There's danger ahead. We need to go. Stay true to yourself."

The teal flames diminished first, and the smoke held an image of an abstraction that looked like a cave before it too disappeared. What was that? Was it where the "ancestors" were staying? She still had a lot of questions for them.

She glanced at her smart bracelet and saw that it was six in the evening. Holy cow! Five hours just vanished. Had she entered a different dimension without knowing? She recalled Grandma Ova had said smoke could travel into the unseen world. Had it taken her there just now? Was that why she'd seen and heard strange things?

A knock sounded on her door, and she jumped.

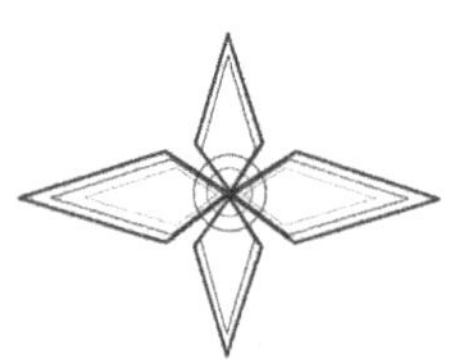

TWENTY

RITA's smart bracelet buzzed from Jarzell's message. *Where are you?*

What did he mean? She checked the previous message and understood. *I'm at your door. Can you open?*

Her brows pushed together as she rushed to open the door. Apparently, she had been wrapped inside another world; she didn't even hear or feel the buzz of her smart bracelet.

Jarzell stood wearing a fresh change of clothes. Fatigue weighed on his body.

"Hi, you look tired. Come in." Rita stepped aside, let him in, and closed the door behind her.

"It's been an interesting day." Jarzell walked into the living room, stared at the metal plate. He sniffed the cedar that filled the room.

Rita picked up the plate, cauldron, and the container of dry Saedo leaves and stored them away.

Rita couldn't think of any other day that could compare to the discoveries she'd acquired in the last twenty-four hours.

"What happened? Want to talk to about it?" She placed a gentle hand on his arm. She didn't know why she needed to touch him. Maybe it was to confirm he was truly home and safe.

"I'm sorry I didn't have time to reply to your messages." Jarzell squeezed her hand. "We destroyed two more dark wells and five Ulkrin hybrid beasts."

"Have a seat first. Then you can tell me." Rita led him over to the couch. "Did anyone get hurt?"

Jarzell shook his head. "Chief Mozar activated the Defendums when Saedo experienced the last storm. The drones are prototypes the government has been working on for a while. Anyway, they proved themselves today when they detected foreign energy within the land, and that's how my brothers could locate the dark well."

"How did the Defendums do that?"

"They fly around and monitor the energy fields around Saedo. When they pick up something off or abnormal, they notify central control. Raeko had been in the office when the alert came in, so he reviewed the data with the engineers and scientists. The Defendums will monitor the land overnight."

Knowing there was something watching for danger settled Rita's nerves.

"We also killed another mother beast. It seems like more are hiding in Saedo. We have to lure them out and kill them. They're breeding more beasts, and that darkness feeds into the dark well, making them easier to form." Jarzell rolled his shoulders and cracked his neck. "As soon as I finished, I rushed home, showered to get rid of the blood and filth, and came here."

"I missed you." Rita grabbed his face and kissed him. Her heart drummed as need pulsed in her core. His tongue didn't act like it was tired. In fact, he kissed with so much intensity and desire that she moaned against his mouth.

He broke the kiss, looking at her. "I missed you too."

She smiled. "You don't kiss like you're tired."

"That's because you energize me." He looked at the empty spot on the rug. "What did you do while I was away?"

Where should she begin? It seemed like she'd traveled into another world and gained several lessons on Saedo lore, but those things could wait.

What Jarzell needed right now was to relax; something to take his mind off of the violence, blood, and death. Everyone had to refill the energy they'd exerted in order to function, including her. He was a soldier who was used to battles, but that didn't mean he didn't need some tender loving care.

It was time to start Rita's creative idea. It would help clear her mind, shove all the concerns to one side for now. Tomorrow, she could sit down with him and review all the clues to where the Sacred Tablet might be. She'd absorbed too much information today. She had to let the dust settle.

"I was inspired to paint again, so I got some supplies." She flicked him a mischievous look.

The gray eyes gleamed. "What's on your mind?"

"Something artistic... something 'messy.' Something I haven't done in a long time. You offered me your services, remember?"

Suspicion flickered in his eyes. "Yes..."

"You inspired me to create something again. But I need your help. It could take hours."

A wide smile stretched on his face. "With that sales pitch, I'm sold. What do you need, Creatress?" His finger traced her bottom lip, and tingles ran up and down her spine.

Rita opened her mouth and took in his index finger. "Are you sure you're up for this?" She continued toying with his finger, and his breathing became uneven. "If you're exhausted, we can wait until—"

"What exhaustion? You've got me hot and bothered. I don't want to wait."

Rita laughed and released his finger. He gasped with disappointment, and she pushed herself up from the couch.

"You can't just tease me like that and leave. I'm too aroused." Sheer disappointment splashed on his face, making him more adorable than before.

"Hold on. I'm prepping my supplies. In the meantime, I need you naked on the couch. Can you move the coffee table aside? I need a full view so I can paint you."

"Whaaat?" He froze with the most shocking expression she'd ever seen on him.

Rita beamed. "Don't back out on me now. You're my muse. My *first* painting on this planet."

"Do I get to keep it?"

"I'm gifting it to you. You can do whatever you want with it."

She hadn't decided exactly how she would paint him. She'd let the paint and the brush guide her. When she painted, her mind shut down, and her heart took over. The result usually surprised her in the most splendid way.

In minutes, Rita returned with her supplies and stared at Jarzell lying on her couch with a hand propped on his head. Heat jolted from her core, spreading through her body. She dropped the bag of supplies on the floor, and the paint tubes fell out.

Jarzell grinned and sat up. "You like what you're seeing? I've never modeled before, especially in the nude. Do human males do this a lot?"

Unable to speak, Rita nodded as her eyes surveyed the ripped muscles on his chest, arms, legs, and abdomen. He was a fine art sculpture. When they made love outside on Grandma Ova's deck, the light was dim, creating a romantic ambience. Right now, the light in her apartment was bright. She could see everything, and everything teased and taunted her body.

"How many men have you seen naked? How many have you painted?" Jealousy coated his words.

"I've painted several naked men, but that was for my art class. Their bodies aren't like yours though." She remembered the models who were fully nude all around to allow her to learn shadows and light. This session with Jarzell was for her pleasure and to commemorate an extra step in her life. "They didn't attract me. Besides, you're the first one I'm gifting an original painting to."

"The first and the *only*. I don't want to imagine you looking at another male like this. Or even painting him." He rose and walked over to her. "Promise me that, and I'll model for you anytime, any day, anywhere. I'll do anything for you."

Heat pulsed from his body, and the teal mist emerged from him like it also wanted to witness this unique painting.

"I don't want you looking at another female the way you look at me now," she said.

He yanked her to him. "I haven't looked at another female since you came into my life. I didn't know why I was never interested in other female star-beings." His hands wrapped around her back, sliding down to her butt cheeks. "But now I know for certain. It was you. Since I rescued you—noticed you— something shifted in me. I didn't want anyone else. When I saw you at the Village Library, I had the feeling you were meant for me."

Rita had to ask the question that had been bugging her. "Are you interested in a long-term relationship with me or are you looking at this as a fun... vacation." She couldn't think of a better word.

A crease developed on his forehead. "I'm only interested in forever with you." His arms drew her closer, and the hard ridge of his arousal pressed into her. "I felt this before you even acknowledged that you saw my mist. Deep down, I hoped you would see it. And you did."

Elation coursed through her. The room seemed to disappear, leaving only them. "So you offered to help repair the windows because of that 'feeling' or because you truly wanted to help?"

"Both. I just needed to be close to you. Know you. Make you mine." He tipped up her chin and kissed her. "Does that satisfy your demands, Goddess?"

Rita palmed his erection and squeezed. "It does. Consider this a deal." She gripped his manhood like a handshake. *Holy shit.* Did she really just do that? Her cheeks were probably redder than the tube of red paint on the floor, but she didn't care.

He roared with laughter. "That's a first for me." He stared down at her hand, clutching his length. "I like your idea of how we seal the deal. I love your 'contract' style."

Embarrassed, Rita pointed to the couch. "You, back over there." She kept her eyes on his fine ass. An artist had to take in all the details to ensure a masterpiece.

Jarzell's grin remained as he resumed his position on the couch with one elbow propped up.

Rita held up a finger. "Don't move. I'm going to set up now." She should've done that earlier, but he'd distracted her. His presence affected her more than she realized. She pressed a button on her state-of-the-art easel and metal limbs and panels shifted to form a side table. She picked the scattered tubes of paint and lined them up on the side table. This robotic easel enabled her to paint on various sized canvasses. On Earth, it was a hassle to accommodate a large painting. Most times, she had to switch easels. This cutting-edge easel also collected paint drips that kept the floor clean. But she placed a large rag under it anyway, just in case.

She sensed Jarzell's eyes on her as she moved, and heat pooled at her center. But she had to focus on her art, not her body. He continued studying her. She'd never had a subject stare at her like that, but she didn't care. She was the Creatress, so she was studying him in more ways than one.

She dropped a paintbrush and bent down to pick it up. She took her time getting back up, giving him a peek at her bosom. Since he was displaying himself to her, it was only fair that he got something extra too.

Rita placed a spare canvas against the wall in case she needed to start over. She squeezed out some paints onto her color palette and grabbed the innovative paintbrush that could switch easily to different types of brushes from flat, round, angled, fan to the mop.

"Ready?" She waved the brush at him.

"Been ready for you, Goddess." He winked and his length twitched as if winking too. This was going to be an interesting painting session.

Rita smiled and turned her attention to the canvas. She inhaled and exhaled slowly, dropping into the moment—into the space of creation where her mind turned off.

Heat caressed her skin, and the scent of cedrus flowed into the room.

She mixed green and navy blue paint to achieve his dark green skin, but then decided this was art. It didn't need to reflect reality. He could be any color. With that thought, the innovative paint sensed her emotion and transformed the paint into a beautiful teal color. She added more colors to showcase light and shadow. Grandma Ova had given her a translucent paint that added a muted sparkle for accent. The sparkles lifted from the canvas surface like swimming stars.

Jarzell couldn't see the painting from his position, which was a good thing because it would distract him. His distraction would interfere with her concentration. She stepped back from the painting, studying it. Sometimes, when she was too close to something, she couldn't see the complete picture. She remembered her teacher reminding her to step back to give the eyes a different perspective. Just like art, there were moments in life that required her to pause and reevaluate.

She moved a few more steps away, angling her head this way and that way with the paintbrush still in her hand. "Wow." She'd always admired the abstract art of Georgia O'Keefe, and she could see a hint of her influence in this painting.

Rita wasn't the type to boast about her own work, but this one deserved it. This was her best work to date. Somehow, her hand worked with the paintbrush and manifested this gorgeous composition with a perfect combination of light and shadow. The artwork highlighted Jarzell's muscular body in an elegant and seductive way. It was a masterpiece that could be displayed in a public room if he wanted that. At first, she feared the painting might be too provocative, but the result astounded her.

"Come here." Jarzell's husky voice broke through the silence in the room.

TWENTY-ONE

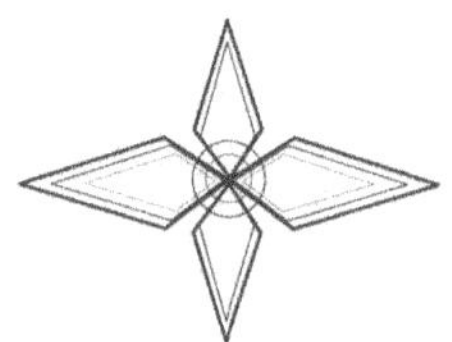

Rita severed the connection with her painting and glanced over at Jarzell.

Bad idea.

He had her attention, all right. His hand was busy with his manhood while his eyes intensified on hers. "You're turning me on, Goddess. I'm laying here imagining you *imagining* me. You don't know what that does to a man who's extremely attracted to you."

Rita placed her paintbrush and the color palette on the table.

"Can I see it?" he asked. "I want to know what I look like through your artistic eyes."

She swerved the easel to face him, and his stroking stopped. He rose from the couch for a closer look.

"I look good. Wow." He cupped her chin in his hand. "I've never seen anything like it, and I'm not saying that because it's a painting of me. The way you painted it, the subject in the painting could be anyone. That's the beauty of it, and it's not as risqué as I expected."

She liked how comfortable he was standing naked in her

apartment, reviewing her work as if it was a part of his normal routine.

He crossed his arms and angled his head, admiring it. "I was thinking it would go into my bedroom where you and I can admire it before we sleep. But now, this is going to be the focal point of my living room." He kissed her, his mouth skimming along her jaw and igniting all kinds of nerves. "I think you should paint more like this and sell them."

Rita placed a hand over his chest. "Maybe. An artist's lifestyle can be unstable in terms of finances. I had a lot of artist friends who could barely pay their bills. It's a hit-or-miss type of thing. You need to find the right collector for you work. That's the key. Art is subjective."

He placed a hand on either side of her head. "I'm telling you, your work is a breath of fresh air here. It's different from anything I've seen. I'm a fan, and I was never into art. You've shown me a new way of looking at things."

How could she not believe him? The way his gray eyes gleamed with conviction could make her believe that there was a third sun emerging in this galaxy. No one had ever believed in her that much. She beat back the tears that wanted to come.

"Why do you believe in me so much?" she asked.

He took her hand and kissed it. "Because I see talent. I see someone who pushed her creativity into a dark corner because of life's troubles, and I want to remind you that you have the skill. You're sharing it with me. Now, share it with others." He placed her palm over his chest. "Most of all, you speak to my corra, and how can I not believe in my corra?"

Teal mist snaked all over the room. White smoke emerged from the pores of her skin and joined the teal, creating an aqua vapor that surrounded them. Three vapors moved around the room.

The vapors floated over to the painting and entered it,

coming out the other side. As they did so, the paint moved fluidly in a manner that maintained the composition, and at the same time, altered the tone of the colors.

"What's happening?" Rita asked.

"Something spectacular." Jarzell gawked at the bizarre image in front of them.

Rita couldn't believe her eyes. This was innovative art. A thought entered her mind and told her to "guide" the vapors.

She took the spare canvas that leaned against the wall and painted a quick abstraction. With her mind, she connected to the vapors. *Join me. Create with me.*

Instantly, the white smoke and the aqua vapors ribboned over to the new canvas and entered the wet paint.

She turned to Jarzell. "Try something with me?"

He nodded.

"With your mind, connect to your teal mist and ask it to join you in creating this new artwork with me. We can connect to it. I can't guide the teal mist because that's your energy, but I can do it with the white smoke and the aqua. The aqua is both of our energies."

If she was a paint color, she was the white and Jarzell was the teal. When they blended, the aqua color formed.

Jarzell waved a hand like a paint brush, guiding his teal mist to create. "This is flekken unbelievable."

They created art together in an incredible new way. "We're both artists now. You are a Creator." Her eyes raked down his body in a lazy perusal, emboldening her. "I've got some paint I want to try."

He flicked her a gaze. "Okay. Do you need a new canvas? This is another masterpiece we just created. I can't believe I painted something. Well, sort of."

"It's an abstraction, so it doesn't need to look like anything.

As long as the colors are pretty together, people will love it. I already love it."

"Okay, let's start a new one." He paused a moment and laughed. "I've never modeled in the nude and I've never painted in the nude, either. Woman, you're introducing me to a provocative world that I don't want to leave."

Rita laughed. "Well then, you're going to love this. I'm going to paint on your body. It's edible paint."

"Oh." His eyes widened as a smirk slid on his sexy lips. "Ohhh. Then that means I can paint you too."

"Yes, you can. This is the 'messy' I've been referring to. We need to stay on this rag." Rita took a small tube of edible paint from the bag and squeezed some on to his body. With her hand, she moved the paint around. His arousal hardened, and she gripped him, adding purple paint to his green stalk. The purple and green created a lovely image. Saliva pooled in her mouth from the look of his erection.

Jarzell sucked in a breath as he removed her top. "I want to lather you up and lick the paint off your body."

In seconds, she tossed her pants and underwear aside, standing naked before him. He pulled her flush against him, and her hands moved the paint around his back, to areas she wanted to nibble. She'd never done anything like this, and it thrilled her. She marked his body with her signature and traced patterns on his skin.

Before she knew it, Jarzell had her on her back with blue paint on her breasts and stomach. He painted her breasts with his mouth and tongue. The orange tip of his tongue had specks of blue. "So tasty, so tangy, so lovely. I'm going to take my time savoring you."

Had she finally converted her impatient man to be patient? She had to remind him about this moment later on. Right now, she wanted to feel everything.

She moaned, wanting more and more of his mouth on her. He cruised his lips to hers, and his tongue entered, tangling with hers. The paint was sweet, but she also tasted a flavor that was uniquely him. Desire zipped through her body, igniting an internal fire that was wild and free.

There would be no one else for her. No one could make her heart beat this fast and want so much. With every kiss he offered, her heart swelled even more. With him, she was free to be herself. Free to create. Free to make a beautiful mess. Free, flawed, and loving it.

Heat radiated from her, and the muscles on her back expanded and tightened as if they agreed too.

She cried out in pleasure when his mouth returned to torment her breasts. She dug her paint-covered fingers into his hair, urging him on. This man knew how to please a woman.

"You're an artist when it comes to lovemaking," she said.

"Only with you. Only for you." The vein on his neck throbbed, and the purple paint that had adjusted to his body temperature fluctuated to red, orange, and yellow. He was modern art, indeed.

Jarzell covered his fingers with gold paint that not only sparkled, but it also had sensory properties that tingled and added heat. The tingles and heat raced across her skin as he painted wavy designs up and down her legs to the inner thighs, settling at her core. *Holy fuck.*

A bonfire of sensations erupted in her. He nudged her knees up and thighs out. With one hand, he lifted her buttocks for a full view of her center. She should be embarrassed, but she wasn't. She loved the way he cherished her; the way he studied her like she was a masterpiece. She almost came from the hungry look on his face.

"I'm painting this flower. This is *mine*." Jarzell sounded like an animal staking his claim. His fingers tantalized her with slow and seductive movements that had her chest heaving. She lifted her head, watching him paint designs on her. Her thighs quivered with excitement. From his angle, what did the art look like?

Pleasure spiraled out of control. When his mouth replaced his fingers, she jerked from the onslaught of bliss. Her inner muscles constricted with delight. Her head fell back to the floor, and she surrendered to his mouth and tongue. The rapture pushed her sexual need higher and higher until she was tiptoeing on the edge.

"You're even more delicious without the paint." He growled and feasted until her thighs quaked, and she whimpered, wanting more from him.

She couldn't hold on anymore. The wave of pleasure matched the urgency of his mouth. She arched into him as the tidal wave of pleasure rippled through her. "Jarzell!"

He gripped her hips and increased his pace, as if he wanted to savor every drop of bliss from her. Finally, he kissed his way up to her mouth. "I love the way you taste. I love how you react to me."

And I love you. That admission set her free. This man was hers. But she wasn't ready to tell him yet. The tidal wave of love needed time to settle.

"You're a beast," she said instead.

He let out a laugh. "Thank you."

Flakes from the purple and blue paint floated from his body and dissolved into the air. This was another reason why she loved the inventions on this planet. When she saw the edible paint at the store, she wasn't sure what the description meant about it dissolving. But after experimenting with this modern paint, she wanted more. She'd have to stop by Spark Your Imagination again soon. What other cool paints were available? Now she wanted to try them all. She imagined what she could do with those high-tech paints. If she was making a debut as an artist in Saedo, then this was the way to go. This modern method would expand her creativity to new levels, both in public and private.

Jarzell positioned himself between her legs. "Do you want me to use the Safe-Sex Spray?"

She had a bottle in her bedroom. But she didn't want any barrier between them. Not now, not ever.

"No."

"Good. Because I want to feel you wrapped around me." He placed his erection at her center, teasing her. "Look at us. We're sexy art." He slid into her slowly. "Making sexier art." He growled as his thrusts deepened. "So flekken sexy." He lowered himself down to press against her.

She shifted, grinding her hips in a way that blended the blue paint on her body to his purple paint. "You've got amazing talent." She moaned as he plunged again.

After a brief break, they created another artwork on a new canvas with their joined bodies. Rita smiled at the artistic collection they were creating.

What should she title this collection?

TWENTY-TWO

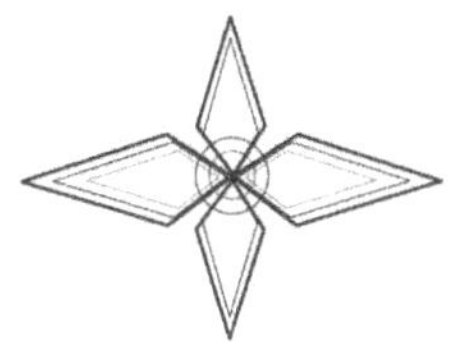

Later that night, Rita woke from a noise.

Jarzell was speaking to someone in the living room. Rita walked into the hallway, just enough to see a virtual screen with a beautiful yellow-haired female star-being. Rita recognized her from The Crystalline SiSTARS Café, where the female star-being had sat behind them with her friends.

Who was she? If Jarzell knew her, then why hadn't he said anything that day?

"I made a mistake. I miss you, Jarzell." Her voice slurred as tears streamed down her face.

Rita's heart dropped to her stomach.

"Where's your sister?" Jarzell asked. "You should go home. It's late, and it's dangerous outside."

"I'm not going anywhere. I just want you with me." The female gulped down something from a bottle and clicked off the screen.

"Flekken!" he shouted.

Rita tiptoed back to bed, pretending to sleep. She heard Jarzell walk in, probably to check on her. Then she heard the rustling of clothes.

Where was he going at this hour? It was midnight. Who was this female? Was she a former lover? Why were they chatting at this time?

Self-doubts made their way to Rita's mind. They had made love just hours ago, and he told her he only wanted her. Was that a lie? She could almost hear the cracking of her heart, creating an earthquake inside her. But she willed herself to be strong. If he was cheating on her, then she needed to see it with her own eyes.

When Rita heard the door click, she jumped out of bed and threw on a top and pants. Jarzell got into his sports rider and drove off. Rita followed in her personal rider, keeping her distance. The roads were busy even at this hour because he was heading into a business section that was open twenty-four hours. He pulled into a parking spot and got out.

Rita followed him and stood behind an advertising panel. Jarzell walked to a bench where the female star-being who'd called him sat by herself. She glanced up, threw her arms around him and kissed his face. Rita turned away as her heart shriveled like a dried flower. She couldn't look at them anymore. His betrayal stabbed into her, and her chest tightened to where she had to brace the panel for balance. Hot tears burned her eyes, and she let them fall.

"Are you okay?" A concerned star-being with orange hair stopped with his mate and checked on Rita. "You look sick."

"I'm okay, thank you." She debated confronting Jarzell. But what for? That wouldn't make her feel any better.

Rita heard the female star-being shout— "Where are you going, Jarzell?"—as she rushed back to her personal rider. Rita didn't know where Jarzell was going, and she didn't care. She just wanted to get away from them, go home, and lock her door.

"Rita!" Jarzell called after her.

She glanced over her shoulder and met Jarzell's shocked

expression. She shot him a lethal warning—for him to stay away. Or she'd detonate her wrath on him. Saying nothing, she whirled around, leaving him and whatever they had together behind.

She wasn't in the mood to talk. She wasn't in the mood for excuses. She was done with the male species. She should've known better.

Inside her personal rider, her body trembled. As Rita stopped at a set of lights, she took several deep breaths to calm her body. From the corner of her eye, she could see white smoke floating in an area in front of her. A strong sensation bypassed her pounding pain, nudging her to investigate. She pulled into a spot under a tree, got out, and walked past the lamp post. Twenty feet away, a dark well swirled, nearly hidden by the shadow of the trees. From her angle, she saw the reflection of dim light on the whirlpool's surface.

She glanced around, but there was nobody in sight. Rita snapped a picture of the well and sent it to the emergency number. A flying robotic thing hovered above the well.

Was that the Defendum spy Jarzell had spoken about earlier? Would he receive the message from this alert? Did it matter? She should stop thinking about him. He was probably still with the female star-being, consoling her from whatever drama she was involved in.

The area wasn't completely dark because of the solar lamp posts and benches along the sidewalk. But the sections with trees were mostly dark, and that was where she stood.

A growl echoed in the night, and her stomach lurched.

Rita had no weapon. How would she defend herself if those hybrid creatures attacked her again? White smoke and a familiar cedrus scent emerged from her body. If she could guide the smoke like she did during her painting session, then she could do it now.

With her mind, she commanded the smoke to multiply. She focused on the cedrus scent. *Amplify. Increase your potency.*

More growls emerged as a mother beast jumped in front of her. Rita stumbled back as fear gripped her. But this wasn't her first time seeing one of these creatures. So the shock factor wasn't as powerful.

White smoke increased around her, creating a white blanket on the ground and in the air. Choking sounds erupted, followed by the cries of the offspring.

"Stop the smoke now!" The mother beast roared.

"No." Rita squared her shoulders and increased the smoke even more.

There was a glow to the smoke that hadn't occurred before. She didn't have time to contemplate that as the mother beast charged at her.

Rita didn't know how she knew what to do, but she reached out and grabbed a stream of the smoke. The contact sizzled her skin, sending a jolt of power coursing through her body. Her body felt light and nimble, almost airy. The logic of what she was doing didn't make sense at all, because how could she grab onto a vapor?

But she had.

She held the stream in her hand like it was a solid rope and she whipped it at the mother beast. Rita's body moved with a fluid motion, flowing with the action rather than against it.

The rope of smoke slashed at the mother beast's body, and her skin singed and bled. The creature howled so loudly, Rita swore the entire village could have heard it. Two more mother beasts appeared, dripping with black water, looking like tar. They must have come out of the dark well.

"Kill her. She's creating the poisonous vapors," the injured mother beast shouted to her peers.

The two newcomers charged at Rita, but then blasts

pummeled their bodies. Rita took the opportunity and whipped the cedrus-scented smoke into them. The rope of smoke slammed into one of their heads and cut it in two.

Shit. Gross. The gore of it froze Rita for a moment. The strong metallic smell of blood rose in the air, twisting her stomach.

Several more blasts destroyed the beast's head and body.

"Rita! Are you okay?" Jarzell's hand tapped on her shoulder.

She glared at him, anger and betrayal still clinging to her. Concern weighed on his face. She stepped away from him, forcing his hand to drop from her shoulder. "Not really."

Was she referring to how he smashed her heart or the fact that she just cleaved a creature's head in half? Did it matter?

Pain flickered in his eyes. She shouldn't care.

"I'll explain everything later," he said, blasting his weapon at more creatures that emerged.

"No need to." Rita continued whipping her smoke rope at the beasts. The muscles in her arms should be tired, but she moved with ease. Out of nowhere, one of the creatures jumped at her, but her reflexes had her body bending back like she was performing some impossible acrobatic move, dodging the attack. How in hell had she bent like that? When she regained her composure, she belted the enemies with her smoke. Even Jarzell shot her a surprised look.

Rita moved closer to the dark well, trying to figure out how to seal it. Smoke and teal mist covered the area. Fortunately, the scented-smoke was harmless to all the Saedo citizens, otherwise she and Jarzell would have been injured before.

Sirens sounded nearby, and she heard Jarzell's brothers arriving in separate emergency autobuses and longships. The foggy atmosphere made it difficult for her to see the creatures and the well now, but she made her way to the dark well, sensing the dark energy pulsing around it.

Energies of violence and darkness crawled on her skin. Something laughed, or was it someone?

When a massive claw with odd patterns on its rough skin reached out from the well and grabbed her leg, Rita fell to the ground and pain shot through her body. It dragged her toward the whirlpool. She held tightly onto the rope of smoke as the claw yanked her closer. White smoke attacked the claw looking like vapory serpents.

"Rita!" Jarzell fired at the claw, and electricity flared from it. Still, it wouldn't let go of her leg as pain throbbed.

As more white smoke wrapped around the claw, the electricity dulled, and a scream echoed somewhere inside the well.

Another glance at the patterns on the claw connected with something in Rita's mind. She'd seen those abstract patterns before, formed by the smoke when they were at Grandma Ova's house. This was the clue. *Nature speaks in metaphors.* Grandma Ova's words sounded in her mind.

Was that a sign that whoever the claw belonged to was the person—or being—creating the dark wells? Rita followed her hunch, but she needed Jarzell's help. Despite what had just occurred between them, he was a good soldier. And he had saved her life in the forest. She held onto those thoughts as they battled these awful creatures. What happened after they were free was another story.

The claw twisted away from the white smoke and reached for her again. Instead of scooting away, Rita moved closer to it. The only way to kill this thing was to find out who it was.

She met Jarzell's eyes. "Do you trust me?" It was an odd question to ask given their situation, but she wasn't referring to their personal relationship.

"I do."

"Then we need to kill that thing with the claw." Another claw reached out of the dark well, gripped her ankle, dragging her body over the dirt and rocks toward the dark well. Pain flared on her back and ankle.

Then heat coursed through her as Jarzell grabbed a hold of her body with both of his arms. White smoke and teal mist enveloped them as they both tumbled into the dark well.

TWENTY-THREE

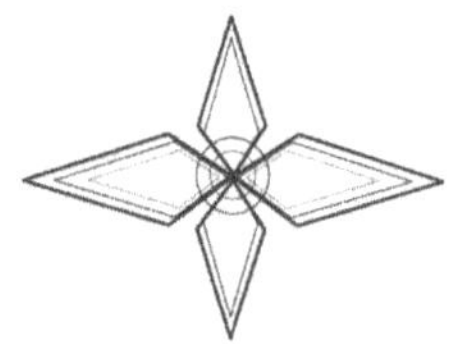

JARZELL'S HANDS embraced her as they tumbled through some kind of tunnel that smelled of death and decay. She couldn't hear anything except Jarzell's heartbeat. It pounded against her body, and that brought to the surface several emotions she was afraid to feel. She shoved them aside as she focused on the threat at hand.

Darkness surrounded them as the spinning sensation quickened, making her nauseous. The spinning slowed as the glow of the white smoke and teal mist illuminated the area, giving them just enough light to see a brown ground was near. The smoke and mist wrapped around her and Jarzell, ensuring their safe landing like magical parachutes.

When her feet touched the ground, she examined herself and Jarzell. Since they dove into the well, she expected wet and gooey water all over her, but her clothes were dry.

"Where are we?" she asked.

Immediately, the opacity of the dark surrounding became translucent, revealing her apartment. She walked around reviewing her living room and the rest of her apartment. Everything was exactly how she had left it. The paintings she and

Jarzell had created leaned against the wall, and her sketchbook sat next to her art supplies on the counter. She had wanted to show the sketchbook to Jarzell later today, but now...She shook her head clear of personal emotions.

She ran a hand over the book, but it felt cold and filmy, as if she was behind some veil.

"We're in between worlds," Jarzell said.

"Between the Seen and Unseen," Rita repeated Grandma Ova's words.

"Give me the Sacred Tablet." A menacing voice sounded behind her.

How did it know about the tablet?

Jarzell stepped beside her in seconds. Was his protective stance a soldier's reflex, or did he still care for her? Why was she thinking about this right now? Maybe it was the fact that she could die at this very moment and never know what happened between them?

Jarzell could die too, and that fact clutched her heart. The pain was too much, and she realized loving him had saved her, regardless of how he had treated her. She loved him, even if he didn't love her in return. She was okay with that. Love was a gift, and that gift had given her back her self-worth. It had taught her about strength and survival. And she would use that new awareness to kill this damn beast.

She didn't need anyone to tell her she was a strong and capable woman. She didn't need a man for her to feel worthy. She knew that deep in her bones.

"Where's the tablet?" the voice barked again.

"What tablet? There are tons of tablets in Saedo. You need to be specific." Rita glanced around her apartment, trying to see where the voice was coming from.

It grunted with annoyance. "Don't be coy, human. We sensed its powerful energy."

"Why do you want it?" Jarzell asked, while surveying the room.

The voice let out a mocking laugh. "Saedo citizens don't deserve such fine wisdom. You don't even know what you have. There are codes on that tablet that can escalate Ulkrin evolution. More power, more magic. Before you know it, Saedo and all of planet Celeron will kneel to us."

Rita and Jarzell exchanged a worried glance. Grandma Ova was right, the brighter Saedo became, the more enemies it would attract.

"Who are you?" Rita asked.

"Show us your face and we can negotiate." Jarzell gripped his silver blaster, preparing to defend them both. "Or are you afraid of us?"

That taunt earned Jarzell a grunt. Rita clutched her rope of smoke tighter in preparation for the battle to come.

A misty gray cloud formed before them, revealing a monstrous male face that grew into a body about eight-feet tall. He wore armor that covered his chest and legs. His bare arms revealed the abstract images she'd recognized from the smoke. Though he had Ulkrin aspects like the horns, this alien appeared different, more powerful. "I'm Commander Ooza. Give me the tablet, and I'll spare your lives."

Why do enemies always say stupid things like that? Did he think she'd believe his poisonous promises? She could never believe in the words of an ugly beast with nasty claws that tried to kill her.

"Surrender and we'll spare *your* life," Rita retorted and got a smirk from Jarzell.

Commander Ooza let out a laugh that echoed in her apartment. Of all places, why was she in her apartment? Who or what had brought them there?

"We don't have the tablet," Rita told the truth. "Why are we here? If you want tablets, go to the library or the bookstore."

Jarzell glanced at his wristband, tapping something while his gaze scanned the area behind Commander Ooza. Maybe his brothers needed his help, or something worse was happening elsewhere.

The scent of cedrus intensified. Rita didn't mind the fragrance, but when it was this strong, it gave her a headache. The Commander sniffed, flared his nostrils, and stepped back. The cedrus affected him like it did the other Ulkrin creatures.

"Give me the tablet before I destroy this place. It's here. I feel it. The portal would've taken you back to Agarrek for interrogation, but your energy brought us here." Commander Ooza looked around, searching for the tablet he couldn't see.

The ancestors had told Rita that it was her journey to find it. Had it been hiding in her apartment all this time? But where was it? If it was in plain sight, she had to lure the commander away before he caught sight of it.

"Even if you retrieve it, how do you know you can access it?" Jarzell asked. Grandma Ova said the tablet chose to reveal the information when it wanted to. Was there another way to force the data out?

"We have our own way. This tablet will help improve Ulkrin land." Commander Ooza replied.

"If you stop abducting and killing people, then maybe your land will improve naturally." Rita lifted a shoulder.

"I like your sassy mouth." Commander Ooza licked his fat lips and raked his nasty eyes down her body. "You're going to be my mate."

Jarzell sent a blast into the monster's arm. "No, she's not. She's mine."

Rita tossed a glance at Jarzell. His cheek muscle twitched, and the lethal glare he aimed at the Ulkrin told Rita he still wanted her. Had she misunderstood the situation with him and the female star-being?

A battle broke out in her apartment, in a place between spaces. Four more Ulkrins slammed against the veil that was behind Commander Ooza, trying to get into this magical space. The smoke and mist increased and blocked the screen that allowed the Ulkrins to see their commander.

Commander Ooza opened his claws and dark energy whirled from them as if he was making his own version of the dark well.

Jarzell sent another blast at Commander Ooza. The Commander dodged, whipping dark power back at them.

"We might not make it tonight." Jarzell turned to her. "I just want you to know one thing: I love you."

There was no time to discuss anything. Commander Ooza enlarged himself a few more feet, appearing stronger than before. He tossed a burst of power at Jarzell, sending him flying across her apartment. Jarzell grunted, pushing himself up from the ground.

"Jarzell!" Fear spiked in Rita as couches overturned, tables and chairs broke, and walls cracked.

From the corner of her eye, Rita's sketchbook glowed. But when she blinked, the book disappeared. Then she knew; the Sacred Tablet hid inside her sketchbook.

She rushed over to Jarzell. "Guide the mist and smoke to kill him."

Teal mist and white smoke interlaced in front of them, like a mating of the two vapors becoming one aqua wall of vapor ropes. Their two different worlds fused, mist and smoke, wet and dry, and the surrounding air stilled as if time was suspended in that moment. During that suspension, something pulsed like a heartbeat: something powerful and unseen. The ground shook like an earthquake had traveled through several dimensions.

With two hands, Rita grabbed the ropes of aqua and swung them at Commander Ooza. The aqua vapors had more power than the white smoke alone. The aqua symbolized the union of mist and smoke, the heart-to-heart of Jarzell and Rita. That was how they could kill the monster.

Jarzell clutched the streams of aqua vapors next to her hands. Together, they smashed the powerful ropes into Commander Ooza. He tried blocking with his dark energy, but the aqua vapors cut through the darkness and sliced into his body. His body crumbled to the floor in several pieces before the vapors devoured him, taking his body parts elsewhere. With the enemy's disappearance, the veil lifted from her apartment and placed her back into the "seen" world.

Though silence followed, a strange energy still pulsed in her home. The couches that had overturned, the tables and chairs that were broken, had returned to their normal, intact state as if nothing had happened. Apparently, what happened in that in-between space didn't carry over to this reality? From outside her window, a hint of dawn glowed. It had been a long and interesting night.

"Are you hurt?" Jarzell examined her, worry lines digging into his face.

"No, I'm fine, and you?" She reviewed him and didn't see any injuries.

"On the outside, I'm okay." The sad look on his face stabbed her. Like her, Jarzell crumbled on the inside. "We need to talk. I don't want to lose you." He choked on the last word. "Please."

Rita nodded. "Okay, but let's get the tablet first. I know where it is."

TWENTY-FOUR

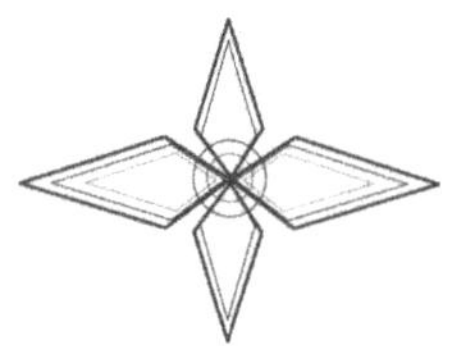

Rita walked to her art supplies, where the sketchbook had returned to its position on the counter. It didn't glow like before, but it didn't need to.

She grabbed it, sensing the heartbeat of the Sacred Tablet in her hands. The book opened itself, revealing the brown glass tablet embedded on the first page filled with sketches of Jarzell's face. The tablet rose up from the page, floating before her. She clasped it, fearing it might drop and shatter.

Warmth and love emanated from the Sacred Tablet.

Jarzell stood beside her, his attention on the sketches. "May I see the book?" he asked.

Rita offered him her sketchbook. She wanted him to see himself through her eyes. He was her muse from the beginning, the start of everything for her. She had rendered him in so many angles and styles, but the one that captured her heart was the gorgeous and realistic figure standing next to her.

"You make me look good," he said, closing the book gently. "I've never been someone's inspiration before. It means a lot to me. Will you continue sketching me?"

"When inspiration strikes."

"I think we should do some self-portraits," he said.

Ideas immediately popped into her mind. "That could be interesting."

His wristband buzzed with a message from one of his brothers. After reading the message, Jarzell looked up. "When we killed Commander Ooza, the dark energy weakened, and that helped Raeko and the others seal up the dark wells around the village. They obliterated five mother beasts and a few squirmurs that crawled out of the whirlpools."

"That's fantastic news!" Relief settled in her, knowing Saedo was safe again.

"It is. Thanks to your help." He brushed his knuckles down her cheek, and she realized she'd missed his touch. "Let's look at the Sacred Tablet and see why it was meant for us."

Rita placed the brown tablet on her kitchen table. A strange light filled in the tablet like some eternal light just switched on. It illuminated the area, and loving energy circulated through the room. When the light dimmed to a soft glow, copper text in hand-written style flowed across the glassy surface. Virtual pages flipped like a book, revealing codes, spells, abstract symbols, and stories. The information reminded her of an encyclopedia full of knowledge. No wonder the Ulkrins wanted this sacred wisdom that could be used to enhance their star race. If Ulkrins became more powerful, then that was a threat to everyone on this planet.

Jarzell took her hand in his. She didn't object as they stared at the flipping pages, wondering when it would stop. The pages stopped at a chapter titled: *Smoke and Mist. A Love Story.*

She read the chapter, or rather, the chapter read itself to her in an ancient voice.

This Sacred Tablet with copper text is the first layer in the Love Spectrum. There are two more layers needed to complete this energy sequence. Smoke and Mist are symbolisms of flexible perception and the ability to enter different realms of existences and beliefs.

Smoke and Mist are fire and water: important elements in nature. Fire and water represent fluidity, malleability, power, light, and life. Fire gives off light; it can dry out water. Water gives life; it can subdue fire. Alone, they are their own power. But when they resonate together as perfect chemistry, a rare loving energy emerges that is gentle, yet potent: smoke and mist. The individuals who achieve this perfection amplify the top layer of the Love Spectrum, and thus, call on the second layer to activate.

The voice continued to narrate the lore. She understood that each of the mist colors her siblings' and their lovers "activated" were part of the top layer of the Love Spectrum. This spectrum was a cosmic energy that the ancestors discovered a long time ago and harnessed in Saedo. Apparently, it had been dormant like a hidden gem. So when her sisters came to Saedo with their unique frequency, the land resonated by the blossoms of blessiums. The flowers were acknowledgements from the land.

Rita remembered how her body had become flexible, malleable when she held onto the ropes of aqua vapors. She'd absorbed their properties and moved like them. She became them in that moment.

"Now, it's making more sense to me," Jarzell said, as the text and voice faded. The tablet revealed what it needed to, and the copper text returned to its unseen realm.

She nodded in agreement as her back itched, and she reached back to scratch it.

"You need a hand?" Jarzell asked.

"Please."

He lifted her shirt and cool air brushed against her skin.

"Oh... this is interesting. Hold still. I'll take a video for you to see."

Jarzell pulled up a virtual screen. Rita gasped at her unscarred back. The burn mark had disappeared. Where did it go?

"I think that scar served its purpose. It brought you here to me. With you by my side, we eliminated our enemies."

"I guess my scars taught me a valuable lesson, that my wounds don't define me. If I hadn't received that scar, I wouldn't have felt rejected, unworthy, or the need to start over. Because of that need, I came here and met you. You loved me despite my scars."

"I love you *because* of your wounds. We all have them. I love the person you became. I admire your strength and persistence. Your wounds only made you more unique and perfect for me. I'm not flawless either."

I deserve a man who loves me for my wounds and for all I aspire to be.

That was the wish she had tossed out to the Universe on that fateful night. The Universe had delivered that and so much more. Rita placed a hand over her thudding heart as gratitude filled her. *Thank you for hearing my prayer.*

A teal flower grew from the glass surface of the tablet. The flower wasn't made of smoke or mist. It was real, with roots sitting on the top.

Rita's eyes widened at the phenomenon. "Are you seeing this? It's a blessium, like the ones Emma, Sasha, Inga, and Vanessa received. Ours is teal."

"Yes, *ours* is teal."

She didn't miss his emphasis. Together, they had created this rare blessium that bloomed with such pretty petals. She recalled her sisters telling her that their buds hadn't fully blossomed yet. She'd have to contact her siblings to see if theirs had changed.

"The Saedo lore is true," Jarzell said. "Our declaration of love gave birth to this flower."

She looked at him, and her heart grew, opening more petals she couldn't see, but felt. Even though she had declared her love for him to herself, she didn't say it to him.

"I haven't really said anything…"

"You don't need to. I feel it. I see it." Jarzell placed his hands on her shoulder. This time, she didn't shove them off. "I love you, Rita. I've wanted to say those words to you, but I was waiting for the right moment. I learned that the 'right moment' is when you feel it, so you don't miss the opportunity to say it. I could've lost you today. I'll never feel this way about anyone but you. You're my true love. My starmate."

Rita swallowed the lump in her throat. Her hands trembled at the question that couldn't wait for later. "Who is she?"

"Yandell, my ex-mate. We're not together. Trust me on that. She wanted to get back together for a while, even before I met you. But I felt nothing for her besides friendship."

"Why did it end between the two of you?"

"Yandell didn't like my impatience, either. She thought I was too rigid and demanded I slow down to appreciate life instead of rushing all the time. The next day, she ended the relationship, saying she'd found someone else." He released a breath. "She never gave me the chance to reevaluate myself. Was I always rushing to do things without keeping her in mind? Probably. Would I have tried to slow down for her? Maybe." He shrugged. "She contacted me last night, crying. She'd been drinking and refused to go home. I knew the Ulkrins were out there, so I was worried about her—as a friend. I didn't want to wake you in the middle of the night for something so trivial, so I snuck out. I would've told you all of this, but you witnessed it instead."

Rita calmed her breathing, and the tightness in her stomach

relaxed. She *had* misunderstood him. "I saw her at The Crystalline SiSTARS Café the day we were there."

"She saw me, waved, and sent me a message, wanting to talk, but I didn't go over to her table," he said. "I think she's suffering from another breakup; I don't know."

"When I saw her clinging to you and kissing you, I couldn't breathe. The betrayal was too much, so I left."

He tipped up her face. "I know. I called Yandell's sister to come get her, and I went after you. The pain on your face crushed me. You matter to me, Rita. I wish I'd handled the situation better. I'm sorry for putting you through that misery. Will you forgive me?"

"You're forgiven." Rita wrapped her arms around him, loving the feel of him against her. Then she veered back. "I know you can be impatient, but that can be a good thing, depending on the situation. Sometimes, a sense of urgency is needed to get things done quickly and efficiently. I've witnessed that in you. But I also think that you can and *should* slow down in certain situations. The same goes for me. I'm usually patient, but I can also be impatient when things aren't done well, and so on. It all comes down to being flexible, and knowing when to run and when to walk." She kissed him on the cheek. "You inspired me to run after my dreams and not sit on them. Sometimes when you wait too long, you miss a golden opportunity."

He embraced her tightly. "And sometimes rushing makes you miss your target."

Rita beamed at her intelligent man. "I love you, Jarzell. I found courage, hope, and my dreams again because of you."

His body shuddered against hers, and his eyes drilled into hers. "I've been waiting to hear those words from you. I've slowed down because of you. You didn't *demand* it from me. You snuck it through me in your own creative way. You teased and tempted me in a way that made me want to slow down. I've got a clever goddess who knows how to manipulate me. I'll have to watch myself."

Rita laughed and loved that he understood her.

He kissed her forehead. "You showed me how wonderful it could be to take my time and enjoy the moment." He moved his mouth over her cheek and down her neck, dropping slow, delicious kisses to her skin that fired up her blood. "You gave me a taste of patience in bed, and in the 'messy' painting session. I loved them all. I never want to rush any of that."

Life had wanted her to understand the journey of her heart. It had taken her time to understand what she wanted—what she needed—and then the courage to face it. When she chose to stay in Saedo, it was her chance for her heart to start anew. From the moment she'd acquired the scars on her back, she was heading here.

The energy of Saedo decalcified her pain, allowing her to love herself, and love a star-being. That love activated the top layer of the Love Spectrum, a cosmic energy that could protect Saedo in more ways than she could ever understand. She might not comprehend everything, but she knew her important role and the roles her sisters played in all of this.

Rita had found the strength to hold on to courage despite the doubts surrounding her. Doubts were the devil that whispered into her ear. Love had drowned out those whispers. Jarzell had shown her what true love was. She found her man on a new planet.

She glanced back at the teal blessium. With her thumb and index finger, she gently clasped the stem of the flower. She retrieved an empty pot from her counter.

"Want to help me? We can plant this together. It's like planting our love."

"I'd be a fool to say no to that. We're sowing our future."

Jarzell clasped his hands over Rita's. Together, they placed the flower into the pot. Dirt filled the pot magically.

In that moment, teal mist and white smoke emerged from the blessium's center, forming a beautiful feminine face.

The misty star-being smiled. "I'm one of the ancestors of this land. The first layer of the Love Spectrum is alive because of you. Thank you. We appreciate your help."

"Thank you for guiding us," Rita said.

"And for watching over the land," Jarzell added.

The ancestor nodded and disappeared as quickly as she came.

Exhaustion tugged at Rita, and she yawned. "We need to return the Sacred Tablet to the Village Library."

Jarzell brought the pot to the window, where the two suns peeked over the horizon, signifying morning was coming soon. "We can do that later, after we rest. Do you need to sleep a bit?"

"I need a shower more. Want to join me?"

"My sense of urgency says yes!"

Rita laughed, dragging him into the shower.

TWENTY-FIVE

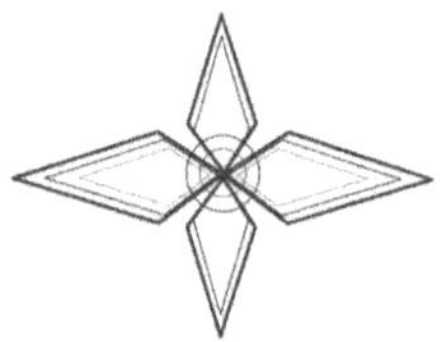

THE NEXT DAY, Rita woke with a note on her nightstand.

I need to run out for a quick meeting. Be back soon.

She glanced at her smart bracelet and the time read ten in the morning. She bolted up and looked out the window. The two suns shone brightly in the blue sky. She was making a habit of waking up late these days. But then again, she'd never fought more monsters than in the last few days. Her body needed the rest.

Rita stretched out her arms, welcoming the new day. She glanced out at the suns again. Their cheerful light brightened her bedroom. There was no hint of battles or any of the darkness that had taken place yesterday. It was like she'd turned a new page in a book.

After the battle yesterday, they had returned the Sacred Tablet to the Village Library. She wanted to visit the other tablets in the coming days. Were they waiting for another couple to find each other, fall in love, and help Saedo? She thought about her sisters, Nina and Isabella. Each of them would have their own journeys and lessons to learn.

Rita washed up and checked on the teal blessium on her

windowsill. The bloom was even larger today. A lovely fragrance emerged from it. She tapped her smart bracelet, snapped a picture of her flower, and sent it to her sisters.

Are your blessiums in full bloom?

She watered the flower and smiled as she pondered on the self-portraits she'd paint with Jarzell later this week. She could try some of her new paints, and Jarzell could practice his growing artistic skills. She had inspired him. But inspiration went both ways.

An idea inserted into her mind. She'd always wanted to paint a collection, a series of art that told a story. Perhaps she could paint a series of abstract paintings that conveyed the love story between her smoke and his mist.

Excitement sparked in her. When was the last time she'd been this thrilled about an art project? She remembered the enthusiasm that creativity used to bring her. It was now back full force. Rita Nelson, the passionate artist, was back. Nothing and no one could stop her vision and desires. And now, she had a warrior by her side.

She was about to go check on the paintings she'd created with Jarzell on that "messy" day, when her bracelet buzzed with messages and images from her sisters.

Emma sent a picture of her yellow bloom. *Mine's in full bloom. It has a lovely scent.*

Sasha's blue blessium looked like the sky. *Isn't this gorgeous? I hope more will grow from this.*

Inga added her red flower, also in full bloom. *I love my flower.*

Vanessa included several angles of hers. *Definitely the most beautiful flower I've seen. We should keep tabs on the flowers' changes. Send each other images when possible.*

These blessiums were messages from the Cosmos. What

Rita and Jarzell had discovered was that the Cosmos spoke in metaphors, and it was up to them to read between the lines.

With every love story, a new energy formed in Saedo, strengthening the land. Love was a blessing, and that blessing was a weapon against any dark forces that wanted to take over Saedo.

A knock sounded on her door, and she knew it was Jarzell by the way her heart galloped. She was sensing his presence more and more. Perhaps that was the connection, the bonding of being starmates.

Rita rushed to open the door. Jarzell wore the most delighted expression she'd ever seen. "Why are you so happy?"

Jarzell stepped inside. "Because I get to see *my love*."

Rita's heart swelled into a happy balloon that immobilized her speech ability.

His words came out with intention, like he wanted her to absorb their power. He looked her square in the eyes. "I love you, and I want you to move in with me. I want us to start a forever relationship. I have a larger space for you to create your art in. You're going to need your own studio."

An art studio sounded lovely, but his eyes held something else. "Why would I need one? The one I have works fine." Rita gestured to her living room.

She went into her storage room to look for the paintings from the other day. They were gone. She whipped a glance at him. "Where are the paintings?"

Jarzell tucked his hands into the front pockets of his high-tech denim and rocked back on his heels. A lopsided grin surfaced on his face. "Well, you gave me one painting. So I took it home and hung it up in your studio."

Warmth filled her even as she narrowed her eyes at him. "Did you really have a meeting this morning? Where are the other paintings?"

He held up his palms. "I had *two* meetings. One was with Chief Mozar and my brothers. We went over a plan to deal with the Ulkrins. We're meeting with one of our allies next week. The Guards of Finntoros who have sworn to help us." With his thumb and index finger, he captured her chin. "The second meeting I had was to do with your dreams. Don't be mad at me, okay?"

Rita arched an eyebrow. What did he do? Nerves stirred in her stomach.

"I took that abstract painting we did together—the one with the help of the mist and smoke—and brought it to the Story Art Gallery. They *loved* it. They want to meet the artist because they want to showcase her work. There's a galactic art exhibit in two months, and they'd love to discuss your participation. This exhibit will be broadcast over the Galacto Net."

Rita stopped breathing. She'd never imagined her art would appear in a gallery, especially that one. The art displayed in their front window always mesmerized her. It had always been a dream to have an exhibit of her work one day. That dream had died when she stopped believing in herself. But now, it was possible. Now, her art was going to be showcased to star-beings, cyborgs, and cosmic creatures all over the Cosmos. Incredible.

Rita tried her best to hold back her tears, but they spilled over. "You believe in me that much?"

"You have exceptional talent. I want everyone to see it and appreciate it. Your work needs to be out there so it can inspire others." He brushed a hand down her cheek. "But I need you to promise me one thing."

She was still trying to grasp the idea of her art collection being viewed by so many star-beings. "What is it?"

"I don't want you painting any nude males besides me. If you need someone to pose for you, it'll be me." His gaze intensified with his *this-is-not negotiable* look.

Rita laughed. "There's no other nude body I want to paint but yours, love. Besides, I'm in the mood for abstraction these days. Something along the lines of smoke and mist."

He kissed her. "I took the liberty of scheduling a time for you to meet with the gallery manager tomorrow. Does that work for you?"

Rita threw her arms around him. "It does. I'll need to cut back my hours at the Village Library to focus on my art now."

"Go for it. Since you're moving in with me, you won't need to pay for housing or utilities. I'll support you. I want to see you succeed."

"We'll support each other. I want your dreams to come true too."

"Finding you, loving you, and making sure you shine your brightest is all I want."

Rita choked up again. "Jarzell..." She had so much to tell him, but she didn't know where to begin. Her love for him and her gratitude for all that he had done for her overwhelmed her.

He pressed a finger to her lips. "You don't need to say anything. I know how you feel. If you want to do something nice for me, I just want a nude painting of you that I can hang next to the one of me."

Rita smiled. "It would be hard for me to pose for myself unless I paint it from a picture--"

"Maybe I can be the artist for a day and see what it's like to stare at a beautiful woman's naked body. My art won't measure up to one you painted of me, but it's one that's personal, and that would be priceless."

Rita tried to imagine how Jarzell would paint her, and it thrilled her. "I'm in a creative mood." She clutched his hand. "Why don't you paint me now?"

A self-assured grin splashed onto his face. "You'll be my newest masterpiece."

She poked at his tummy playfully. "And yes, I'd love to move in with you. I guess impatience is still tugging at you."

Jarzell scooped her up. "Impatience is a flexible friend. It knows I can't wait for us to start our life together."

She rolled her eyes, laughing.

While the lovers prepared for their painting session, the teal mist met up with the yellow, blue, red, and purple mists outside the window and combined their colors into a rainbow ribbon. The rainbow ribbon of energy flowed to the next destination, where it came into contact with the second tablet. A kaleidoscope of colorful energies swirled as the tablet disappeared, sparking the next cycle of love.

Thank you so much for reading! I hope you enjoyed Rita and Jarzell's story. Read Nina and Zeycott's story in **An Alien Spark**. Coming soon! Don't miss out on any new releases. Sign up for my newsletter!

http://callazae.com/newsletter/

If you're curious about Daedriel's story, you can read about him in **Unlock the Angel.** This is the first book in my Seraphim Angel Order Series.

UNLOCK THE ANGEL
EXCERPT

Blurb

His heart is engulfed with the dark… but for her, it awakens with light.

Disheartened with relationships, Cathy Lu concentrates on her career. But the magic around the August Full Moon lures her to a stunning angel who illuminates her desires in a way that makes her wonder if everything is just an illusion.

As a seraph bound to blood, death, and responsibility, Daedriel has never had a long-term lover. But one kiss from Cathy unlocks everything for him, making him want the forever.

Can he keep her safe while evil swarms around them? Or should he keep her away from him, away from all the darkness that threatens him?

Excerpt

Cathy

Cathy Lu hammered a nail into the plank of wood on her back deck and thought about her ex-boyfriend—specifically his family jewels. How would he feel if she pounded him like this nail? Yes, it was a morbid thought, but as an ex-girlfriend who had been betrayed, she had every right to feel that way. Cheaters deserved a painful punishment, didn't they? They had to feel all the pain they'd bestowed on their significant other. That should be a law. So, she envisioned all the things that made her feel better. Wasn't that part of the healing process?

She pounded another nail into the wood and admired her work. She'd learned a few handy things during her two-year relationship with Gavin. He had promised to renovate her deck and the new studio she was adding to her house. But promises from a cheating man rusted over time. It made her wary of men's promises in general. Now, she depended on herself.

Cathy had kicked Gavin out of her home four months ago when she discovered several text messages and emails he'd been sending to two other women. She should have suspected something was up when he came home later than usual or when he had unexpected phone calls that took him into another room. She had been too trusting.

She considered herself an intelligent woman, but when she discovered the truth about Gavin, it made her feel stupid. Love had a way of distorting things, and she couldn't afford another loss like that. She was careful now. She had to be. Her heart had shattered, and she had hammered it back together. She sighed at the symbolism of hurting Gavin and also piecing herself together by hammering a single nail. Maybe that idea could make its way into her new greeting card collection.

Despite it all, she had moved on, mending herself one step at a time. Time spent alone gave her the retrospection and the clarity to focus on her company, Luminous Press. She had a small team of people who worked for her, making sure her journals, novelty books, greeting cards, and other miscellaneous products were delivered on time to their vendors. She and her mother, Celia, had started the company eight years ago, when she was twenty-five years old. Working with her mom had taught her how to be a successful businesswoman and a decent person who looked at things with compassion.

Be gentle to everyone. You never know what someone is going through. You can't measure someone else's pain from a personal scale.

Everything was different when it was personal, wasn't it? The measuring scale changed when you were the one experiencing the pain. It was all perspective. No one could ever understand that misery until they'd experienced it themselves. Standing on the outside made it difficult to see the storm from within.

Her mother's wise words echoed in her mind. If only her mom were still alive, she'd comfort Cathy, reminding her that not all men were the same.

Victor Perez knocked on the glass panel of her sliding door, opened it, and stepped out to the deck. "I'm all done for the day, Cathy. The two bathrooms, kitchen, and living room are all spotless now." He smiled and removed the apron, folding it into his hand.

Cathy rose to her feet and stretched her back. She appreciated his gesture even though she knew that his wife, Rosa, needed him more. Rosa and Victor had been cleaning Cathy's house for the last two years until she fell sick with a thyroid disorder that had gotten worse in the last few months. They had planned on early retirement, but life threw a curveball at them that readjusted their plans. So now, it was just Victor supporting his family. Their daughter, Lizzi, who was also Cathy's friend, lived in New York. She'd come home to visit and assist them whenever she could.

"Do you need me to help you with anything else before I head home?" Victor asked.

The weight of his wife's illness sagged on his face even with that adorable smile. The eyes and facial features revealed a lot of things that people didn't realize.

Cathy tapped the hammer against her hand. "I've got it handled. Thank you, though. Please send my best to Rosa. How's she doing?"

Victor sighed, and his shoulders drooped. "She's improving slowly. Her hair isn't falling out as much now with the new medication. We have a doctor's appointment next Friday to follow up. I'm praying for good news."

Cathy squeezed his arm. "Please keep me posted. Rosa's a strong woman. I'm sure she'll overcome this."

He nodded, giving her a warm smile. "Thank you."

"You don't have to come next week. I'll see you in two weeks," Cathy said and noticed the worry lines on his forehead. "Don't worry. The payment won't change. I figure you could use that time to be with Rosa. Besides, I live here alone. How much of a mess can I possibly make in a week?" She knew most people hired a cleaning service every two weeks, but she kept Victor and Rosa on once a week. She liked them and didn't mind supporting their business. They had been cleaning for her mom before Cathy hired them for her own house.

His eyes watered. "I don't know what to say."

"Say that you'll make the best of it. Life is short, Victor. Be with your family when you can."

After Victor left, Cathy resumed her work. She tried to take the same advice she gave to others, which was why she planned a three-week vacation to regroup. She hadn't taken a break in a long time, so this vacation was a treat. Her best friend, Sydney, the vice president of Luminous Press, could manage while Cathy was away.

Cathy planned on using this extra time to brainstorm the greeting card collections for the next few seasons. Designing the art for the greeting cards was one of the fun parts of her business. It activated a different area in her brain that wasn't crammed with numbers, profit margins, production, deliveries, and so on.

A bird squawked somewhere, and the unique sound broke through the silence. She rose from the deck and glanced toward the woods that drew her to this place. Beyond the trees was the gorgeous Prudent Lake. She had brought a tent out there a few times and slept under the moon and stars. She was due for another adventure soon, especially with the August Moon Festival next week.

When she was six years old, she looked out her bedroom window at the full moon and saw a gold rim around it. It glowed for a while, mesmerizing her. At that time, she had felt a warmth brush against her face when the rim glowed, but it could've been the imagination of a child believing in magic and fairy-tales. Because of that childhood experience, Cathy felt an odd friendship with it. The moon pulled at her in an inexplicable way.

With nature as her background, Cathy found the stability to move on after her mother's death a year ago. They used to come to Prudent Lake on vacation when she was little, so living here was somehow reliving the precious moments they'd shared together. She had no idea where her father had gone. He left when she was six, and that broke her mother.

Another squawk rang out, and she looked around, trying to see the bird or hawk that was making the lovely sound. She spotted nothing. She went into her kitchen, took out the bag of birdseed, and filled her bird feeder. "Enjoy your snacks."

She loved watching the birds gathered in her backyard like it was their playground. The enchanting sounds of nature were the spa that relaxed her.

Her phone rang, and Sydney's name flashed on the screen. "Hey, I don't mean to interrupt your vacation, but I just wanted to remind you about the August Moon Festival next Friday in Boston. Are you going?"

The August Moon Festival was a special time of the year for her family and her heritage. In the past, she'd attend the event with her mother. But this year, Cathy wanted to do something personal, something without the crowd. She could celebrate the holiday right in her backyard.

"I'm going to pass. I'll just do something small at home."

"Are you sure?" Disappointment leaked from Sydney's voice. They had met in college and became fast friends.

Cathy appreciated Sydney's intelligence and foresight when it came to business. Outside of business, Sydney was the trusted friend every woman deserved. Without Sydney's support in both business and friendship, Cathy didn't know if Luminous Press would be as successful as it was.

"Yes, I'm not in the mood for crowds this year."

"Hang out with us girls," Sydney said. "We love talking shit about cheaters, and there's *a lot* of them. That means we'll have plenty of conversations and drinks."

Cathy laughed, appreciating her friend. "We'll hang out soon, I promise. I need to hire a contractor to finish my studio. I want to get it done before I return to work. And I'm brainstorming the new greeting card collection too."

"You're *supposed* to be on vacation," Sydney said with a disapproving tone.

"Yes, *Mom*. I know, I know. I don't mind it, though. The creative part is fun for me. You know that."

"I do, and that's why I'm not driving over there and dragging you away. Do you want me to bring you back any mooncakes, lanterns, food, or anything?"

"No, thanks. I already placed an order for the mooncakes. They're being shipped to me. Have fun, and don't forget to make your wish to the Moon Goddess. You never know. She could make your dreams come true."

"I'll be sure to make a long list for her. She should find something on there to give me," Sydney said.

"You are the queen of lists." Cathy could imagine the several pages of demands from Sydney.

"Hopefully, the Moon Goddess won't find me too high-maintenance. I only want intelligent, sexy, humorous, and thoughtful men to come to my door. I'll even settle for their snores and messiness." She let out an unladylike laugh. "Maybe we're doomed, Cathy. Maybe we're meant to be alone, which I don't mind now and then. But sometimes I miss that connection, you know? What happened to all the decent men who wanted gorgeous women with acute intelligence and creativity?"

"We're not doomed," Cathy reassured her best friend. "We're special, and special things are rare. 'Decent' men are rare too. We just have to wait for our turn. In the meantime, live life. Have fun. The right guy will come along. You're a fabulous catch, and you need someone who measures up to you. Don't ever lower your standards to be with someone."

Though Cathy offered words of encouragement to her friend, a part of her wondered if there was a decent man out there waiting for her. After her failed relationship, it was hard to believe in happily ever after.

"This is why Luminous Press is successful," Sydney said. "You always turn the bitter into beauty. We make fabulous journals and greeting cards that give people hope."

"Hope is the lantern that gives off light when you need it."

Cathy didn't know why these deep thoughts were spewing out of her so easily.

"Oh, I just thought of something!" Sydney said with excitement. "What do you think of these for Valentine's Day cards? *Do you want to be my lantern? I burn for you. Let me light you up! Let's illuminate the night together.*" She giggled. "They're cute and cheesy, but I have a weakness for that stuff."

"I think they're perfect." Cathy grinned into the phone, admiring the creativity of her friend. "I'll let you handle the next Valentine's Day Collection."

"Cute and cheesy, here I come."

Their conversation carried on a few more minutes before Sydney had to run to a meeting.

Cathy tucked her phone into the back pocket of her shorts, picked up the hammer from the deck, and dropped it into the pouch of her tool belt strapped around her waist. She strode over to the unfinished addition on the side of her house, which also shared the same deck. With hands on her hips, she envisioned the complete studio that would allow her more space to create.

Another squawk erupted nearby. Cathy glanced over to the tree next to her just in time to see a splash of glistening white feathers disappear into the woods.

What kind of bird was that? She loved discovering strange animals and rushed down the steps in the hope of catching the bird. Hoping it perched somewhere close for her to peek, Cathy made her way into the woods.

About ten feet in, she didn't see anything and headed back to her deck. As she walked, a strange sensation pulled at her. She wobbled a bit and blamed her imbalance on the lunch she missed. She got caught up with all the hammering. She glanced at her phone; it was already six in the evening. It was time for dinner. *Shit.*

She got back onto the deck and was about to enter her home to make a sandwich when she heard the squawk again. This time, it sounded further away, but the call echoed through the woods like gentle music that penetrated through the clutter of your mind, catching your attention. Not only that, she heard a loud swoosh of wings flapping somewhere. A powerful gust of wind carried an interesting scent to her nose. Was it citrus or sage? She wasn't sure, but she liked the aroma. It soothed her.

She waited a beat to see if she could hear it again, but silence reigned. Was it her imagination? Or was there some large bird out there? Perhaps it was someone's exotic pet that had gotten lost.

She'd investigate after she fed herself.

Daedriel

One flap of wings and he soared across the serene skyline, over dense trees and sparkling lakes, taking in the mesmerizing view of Earth. He glided through the air, letting the wind massage his face and feathers.

In a horizontal position and ten feet above the water, Daedriel glanced at his reflection. Dark hair, a cream T-shirt, black leather pants, and iridescent blue wings glistened against the glassy surface of the lake. His blue feathers darkened from the warm colors of the setting sun. One set of wings flapped and allowed him to soak in the fresh air that invigorated his lungs. The other two sets of wings rested in their invisible state. There was no need to exert more energy than necessary. The air on Earth was denser than that of the Celestial Realm, but his body could transmute the air quality to suit his need.

As a seraph from the twelfth-dimensional matrix, Daedriel possessed power more potent than any other angels—even the Archangels, who were his friends. Well, some of them, anyway.

He smirked, knowing that if they heard him, they'd object and challenge him to a duel until all their feathers were destroyed in the battle. But those days of carefree play amongst friends hadn't been around for a long time. He missed it, but there were important priorities now. The battle to protect the Celestial Realm had intensified and thus tossed all the angels into defensive mode. The threat to their home and their existence hung in the balance as darkness multiplied within the Universe.

The Celestial Realm was a sacred place within the twelfth-dimensional matrix that was also a doorway to higher dimensions. Some he had visited, while others remained a mystery to him because to get there required an energy boost he didn't have. What he possessed allowed him to travel up to the fifteenth-dimensional matrix. His responsibility to rein in the darkness kept him busy enough from the twelfth dimension and below.

The darkness continued to infect and distort the Celestial Realm, which was why he was on Earth trying to locate the traitor, Rask. He had once been a trusted guard, but he stole the Reversal Black Tourmaline, a rare gem infused with darkness. A regular black tourmaline crystal absorbed and neutralized negative energy by turning it into nothingness, giving that energy a new beginning. But dark powers had manipulated one black tourmaline eons ago, reversing its natural abilities. The Reversal Black Tourmaline had absorbed and stored so much dark energy that it became a weapon for the dark side. The dark could pull power from that stone to feed itself.

Years ago, the seraphim angels had won it back from the dark. They brought it to the Auric Circle, where powerful celestial forces extracted the darkness to be alchemized slowly, naturally. To destroy such a powerful gem could wreak havoc on all life forms.

Where was Rask? Daedriel had tracked his energy to this place known as the state of New Hampshire in the United States of America. Of all places, why was Rask here on Earth, in a land filled with trees and lakes? Was Daedriel being misguided? That thought crossed his mind several times, but he trusted his instincts. Something here was calling him, and he had to find out what it was.

As he neared the home he'd just bought two weeks ago, his pet parrot, Tika, flew up to greet him.

"You're late." The white parrot squawked with its purple beak, gliding beside Daedriel. The pair of white wings glistened with a pink hue from the setting sun. "Did you know you have an interesting neighbor? She's human."

"We're on Earth, and humans live here. Aren't you supposed to be watching the energetic screen for any signs of disruption? We have to find Rask and retrieve the Reversal Black Tourmaline."

"I was. But then I heard loud noises in the woods, so I went to check. That's my job, isn't it? I'm supposed to investigate if something doesn't seem normal and notify you."

Daedriel sighed, knowing it could be a long conversation with Tika's ability to talk on and on.

"What did you find out?" Daedriel landed on the balcony of his house and folded back his wings. The modern home was built by an architect and contained all the amenities that were useful for Daedriel. He'd spent an obscene amount of money on the purchase. He needed to be at the center of this place where dark energy pulsed strongly. But there was another unidentified source of energy that called to him.

Daedriel shifted his wings into invisible mode and stared at his parrot. "I'm listening. What did you find out? And be quick about it."

"Well, it was nice seeing you too." The parrot gave him a

look similar to an "eye roll." Tika was a celestial creature that could mimic beings around him.

Exhausted from the hunt for Rask, Daedriel wasn't in the mood to chit-chat. He had flown along the eastern coast, trying to locate his enemy. The fact that Rask could've already used that stone infused with dark energy twisted Daedriel's stomach. He didn't want to think about that catastrophe.

But if Rask had used it, Daedriel would have felt the shock waves. The energetic disruption would have interfered with Earth's frequencies. The release of extreme malice and menace from the Reversal Black Tourmaline would open a gateway for more evil to enter and reproduce on Earth at an exponential rate. The dark energy held within this stone came from dangerous beings that wielded potent powers. Darkness existed everywhere. It knew how to maneuver and manipulate energies to suit its needs. The Reversal Black Tourmaline was the steroid needed to empower itself.

Daedriel couldn't let that happen here on Earth—a place already immersed with so much suffering. On a third-dimensional matrix, Earth was more vulnerable than other planets that existed on a higher frequency. Humans who were weak in their minds and hearts would be affected most. The teeth of evil would sink into them, turning them into willing soldiers to expand cruelties.

Damaat. Where the fuck was Rask?

"I'm tired, Tika. I've been searching for the bastard for two days."

The parrot made a sound and jumped onto Daedriel's shoulder. "We'll find him, Dae."

A noise echoed in the forest, and the vibration caressed Daedriel's skin as if calling him. That caught his attention immediately. Ever since he'd been on the earth plane, he hadn't experienced this odd phenomenon. The energy on Earth was heavy. He had to use more energy to cut through the density here.

He strode toward the edge of the balcony, staring toward the direction of the neighbor he hadn't met. As he honed into this strange force, he recognized a familiar moon aspect. This feminine energy had a connection to the moon.

In all of his immortal life, he hadn't met a being that radiated this kind of moon frequency. Was this the unidentified energy calling him?

"I sense the moon in her—whoever she is," Daedriel said more to himself.

"I know. That's also why I flew over to her house to see what she was doing."

"What was she doing?"

"Hammering at the wooden board on her back deck and mumbling to herself." The parrot flew over to the ledge of the balcony. "Humans are interesting. They're so *dramatic*. Thanks for taking me on this trip to Earth so I can see for myself."

"It's not a vacation, Tika."

"I know. But I'm learning from pure observation. Anyway, there's something different about her. Your senses are better than mine, angel warrior. So I figured I'd let you know so you can acquaint yourself."

"Acquaint myself?"

"You're here to search for Rask. This is Earth, so the playing field is different. Maybe if you make some human friends, they can help us. Then we can go home and resume our lives."

Tika didn't understand that darkness had changed everything, and searching for the traitor was one of many tasks his seraphim brothers and he were doing. But his parrot friend didn't need all the gloomy details. Daedriel wanted hope to continue perching on his friend's soul. Hope was the thing that kept everyone going. Despite how much Daedriel wanted to give Tika the truth, he understood that some truths were best kept hidden for now.

His mind whirled to his human neighbor. Tika was right; Daedriel could use some human assistance.

But how was he supposed to acquaint her?

Read now! **Unlock the Angel**
www.callazae.com/books

ACKNOWLEDGMENTS

Thank you to Laurie, Anna, and Jenny who helped my story shine. You are the shiny siSTARS in my galaxy. Thank you to my family who always give me everything I need to pursue my dreams. You are my entire Universe.

And thank you, dear readers, you give me a reason to keep writing. Without you, there's no one to appreciate the stardust within my creation. You have my utmost gratitude. Thank you, thank you, thank you.

ABOUT THE AUTHOR

CALLA ZAE

Calla Zae writes otherworldly romance. She loves delving into fantastical worlds where her imagination roams wild. Calla is also an artist who enjoys playing with colors, textures, and patterns. She has a love for mysticism, astrology, astronomy, Kdrama, Cdramas, true crime TV shows, romantic suspense novels, cats, and nature.

Calla lives in Massachusetts with her husband who keeps her grounded to Earth and two creative children who think she has her own secret planet. They're onto something...